Back Alley Secrets
in a
Small Southern Town

P J Jennings

NEWMAN SPRINGS PUBLISHING
320 Broad Street
Red Bank, NJ 07701

First originally published by Newman Springs Publishing 2020

ISBN 978-1-64531-866-8 (Paperback)
ISBN 978-1-64531-867-5 (Digital)

Printed in the United States of America

To "Ammie," who taught me to believe in myself
and never give up on my dreams.
To Xan and Ken, who were there to give me
that extra nudge when it was needed.

Chapter 1

Cindy

Ring! Ring! Ring! Ring! Looking at the clock and seeing that it is 3:00 a.m., Brett wondered who could be calling at this hour. Knocking over the lamp as she reached for her cell phone, Brett answered, "Hello," in an irritated sleepy voice. "Hello," she repeats only to hear uncontrollable sobbing.

Finally a voice on the other end screamed, "Cindy is dead! Oh my God! Cindy is dead!"

"Wh…at? Who is this? What did you say?"

Chris Manning, Brett's husband, heard the commotion and woke to hear Brett yelling that Cindy is dead. He was speechless as he reached to comfort his wife. Cindy…dead! Brett dropped the phone in disbelief and began to cry, repeating, "Cindy is dead… Cindy is dead." Chris hugged her as he rocks her back and forth, not knowing what to say or do to ease her pain.

"Brett! Brett Manning!" Finally she picked up the phone and began talking to the person on the other end who she recognizes to be Stephen, a convenient friend of Cindy's when it fits his needs. It would only be fitting that he would be the one contacting her friends. Stephen Jones was a tall dark flamboyant man with long jet-black curly hair which he kept dyed blond. He came out of the closet a couple of years ago which surprised no one. He just stated the obvious. No one really cared. He was still the same *annoying* Stephen. "What happened? Was she in a wreck?"

"No! No!" he yelled. "We were riding around, going nowhere in particular, laughing, talking, and drinking, just chillin'. Out of the clear blue sky, Cindy asked me if my momma was home. I told her yeah. But since it was after eleven at night, I told her that she was probably sleeping. She looked disappointed and said, 'I wanted her to pray for me.' Then she took a deep breath and slumped down in the seat. I kept calling and shaking her, but I didn't get a response. So I took her to the ER. They tried everything, but it was too late… She was gone… Cindy was gone." Loud screaming and yelling filled the phone again. Chris took the phone from my hand and hung it up because he saw that I was in a state of disbelief, not knowing what to say, trying to digest what Stephen had just told me, sitting quietly on my bed, thinking my best friend, the woman who was closer to me than my own sister, was gone. Suddenly it hit me like a ton of bricks, and I just lost it. Crying, not knowing what to do, think, or say, I called Joyce Black.

Before her phone could ring good, she picked up crying, "I know. I can't believe it either." Neither of us knew what we were going to do now. Cindy was the voice of reason. She was the glue that bonds the three of us together.

Sitting in the dark, I was remembering when I first met Cindy. Well, long before meeting her, I had heard about her. Boy, did she sound like a straight up nasty girl. Her full name was Cynthia Denise Porter, but everybody knew her as Cindy. Cindy did this. Cindy did that. Did you see what Cindy had on the other night? I was sure that I was not going to like this Cindy even though she did pique my interest; and according to everybody, she was the "it" girl of this backward hick town. Cindy stood about five feet six with long jet-black coarse hair that flowed down the center of her back. Her complexion dark and she had brown eyes. She was thick with an hourglass shape. It drove men wild. Cindy's mother and father were originally from St. Paul; but since he was a long shore man, he traveled a lot. Cindy and her mother stayed in St. Paul but would visit him from time to time on some holidays and school breaks. Cindy would often talk about the places they would visit as they traveled around the world. Listening to her stories made many of us envious. By the time her father retired and moved back home to St. Paul to live, Cindy had married a man she met during one of her visits with her father and was living in Boston. Shortly after her father retired and moved to St. Paul, Cindy, after ten months of marriage, decided that this was not for her and moved home too. By the next year after her divorce, she was dating several eligible men but only one caught her eye, Nathan Porter. He was a fine statue of a man who just happen to be president of the First Trust Bank of St. Paul, and Cindy had to have him. He was always well-dressed, well-groomed, and his cologne was subtle but manly. It drove the women wild. Cindy was going to have him or bust torment wide open. After many trips to the bank for one reason or another and chance meetings around town, casual conversations, she got her wish, and he asked her out to dinner. They dated for a while, and she soon had his nose wide open. He wined and dined her like no other. They were always with each other and seemed like the perfect couple, happy and in love. No one was surprised when he popped the question. Cindy didn't believe in long engagements, so they were married the following year. The wedding was beautiful, and Cindy was a living doll. They honeymooned in Florence, Italy. When they returned home and you asked Cindy how everything was, she would coo, "Just perfect." They built this beautiful house, and Cindy decorated it to a tee. She was always having dinner parties or little get-togethers to show off her home. It really was a sight to behold. The following year, their daughter, Samantha, was born, and this made Cindy feel that her life was complete. Samantha was a living doll and was the splitting image of her dad, and everyone knew that she was the apple of his eye. Everything seemed to be going great with Cindy and her little family, but for some reason, Cindy was beginning to get restless. Soon Samantha, Sam for short, was starting to spend more and more time with Cindy's parents. Nathan felt that she was spending too much time over there and tried to get Cindy to keep her at home more. He would even take Sam to his mother in Lakeview, South Carolina to visit, but Sam wanted to go to Grandma and Grandpa. She loved Nathan's mother. It's just that she felt more at home with Cindy's parents. But as Sam got older, she loved staying with Nathan's mother, Ma-ma, on the farm in South Carolina, especially since Ma-ma gave Sam her own pony. This made things even better. Cindy loved Sam to death; but when she was with the grandparents and with Nathan attending one meeting after another, this freed up her time and gave her more time to get into devilment.

Chapter 2

Affairs

With too much free time on her hands, Cindy started a flirtation with some of the men around town, nothing serious, just good ole teasing. But there was one that caught her eye. He was one of the sleaziest men in town. Everyone was shocked at her choice; but as I later found out, this was the kind of men that she was most comfortable with. I don't know. Maybe it was because she felt that she wouldn't get involved with them, and she could walk off at any time and not look back. Then there were those that said she was this way because the man she called "daddy" was not her biological father and that her mom had an affair with one of the local ministers, Reverend Brown. Gossip claims that Mr. Smalls was working in Japan when this was supposed to have happened. So he knew that the baby wasn't his, but he loved Mrs. Smalls and went along with it. It was said that when Cindy's mom told him that she was pregnant, he asked how that could be possible when he hadn't been home or seen her in months. Anyway, even though he went along with the lie, he never really treated Cindy as a father would to his own daughter. I always felt that there was some resentment there. Maybe it was because he never had any children of his own. Sometimes I wonder if he ever tried to really accept her as his own. The day Cindy was christened, it was said that the wife of Reverend Brown walked down front, looked at Cindy, and burst out crying. That was validation for everybody that Sunday that the rumors were true. They could not wait to get out of church to get that grapevine news going. The Browns eventually moved to Logan, the town in which I lived and started attending Grove Park United Methodist Church which I am a member of. They would be at church every Sunday and sat on the pew in front of my mother and our family. Momma knew them and always had conversations before or after services. They seemed like a nice couple. About five years after the Browns moved to Logan, Reverend Brown died. Before I knew the story, Cindy would always ask me about Reverend Brown's wife. I really think that she was sorry about what her mother did.

Anyway, Jim, the new man in Cindy's life, was a little taller than her, slender with dreads, didn't work, and was a sloppy town drunk. His mother and Cindy were good friends which I never understood because she was older than Cindy, and they didn't have anything in common except that they were members of the same community Christmas savings club. Jane Kirkland, Mrs. K as she was known around town, thought that she was *the* fashion queen. You never saw her without being dressed to the nines in *whatever* her sister sent her in the box from "up the road," aka New York. She was a short chubby woman who loved her weave and always had it long and swinging down her back, and we never knew what color it would be from week to week. She would cover up for her son and Cindy and would even let them meet at her house. Now this woman was the biggest gossip in town and would tell everything, including her son going with Nathan's wife which she felt like it was something big. Cindy knew this but—well, Cindy had gotten comfortable, stupid, or just didn't care because she would leave work and meet him at her house. Yes, you heard it right, at her house. Some seem to think that this is what ticked Nathan off. Oh, did I forget to mention that Cindy was the principal of the elementary school in the next town which was eight miles away. Of course, Jim's mother was going to spread this. The principal going out with her son. She made sure that every man, woman, and child knew that tidbit of news and made sure that it was the talk of the town. Well, enough was enough. Nathan got tired of the gossiping behind his back and decided to do something about it. Nathan Porter was a little taller than Cindy and had a built out of this world. He was a quiet, kind person who would go out of his way to help a person in need. But there were a few people that mistook his kindness for weakness, and evidently his wife was one of them.

Nathan began watching and following his wife. When he had gotten enough information and evidence to plot his revenge, he put his plan in motion. One morning, he told Cindy that he had a conference to attend out of town. So Cindy seized this opportunity for a booty call at her house. She went to work as usual but didn't stay. When Nathan called her office, her secretary told him that she said she wasn't feeling well and needed to go home. Everything was falling into place.

His plan had worked. Jim was already there, sitting in the swing in the backyard, waiting with anticipation. It wasn't long before Cindy was turning into her driveway. He walked toward the car as she pulled into the driveway. She got out of the car, unlocked and opened the backdoor. Before they could get inside, good they were tugging at each other's clothes. They retreated to the bedroom and began their midmorning tryst. As they got deep into their sexual frenzy and when both were at the point of erupting into total ecstasy, so much so that neither one heard the backdoor open, in walks Nathan carrying a rifle and stands in the bedroom door. When the two of them finally saw the reflection of a shadow standing in the door and realizing who it was—I'm sure more than their love juices were flowing on the sheets—"Oh shit!" they yelled almost in unison. Nathan just stood there with this funny look on his face. Then he pointed the gun at Jim and didn't say a word. Jim jumped out of the bed, getting tangled in the sheets and falls to the floor, crying, "Please don't shoot me. Please don't shoot me!"

Nathan let him plead and beg for a few minutes. Then he looked at him, laughed, and said, "I wouldn't waste my time killing something like you. Now get the fuck out of my damn house." Jim left naked, scared, and running for his life with what clothes he could grab in his hands. What a sight that must have been! By this time, Cindy was crouched in a corner of the bed in shock and disbelief, not knowing what to do or say. To add pain to her shame, Nathan just looked at her, shook his head, and walked away laughing. Well, that made Nathan's day, and he told everybody what happened, how Jim, naked on the floor, begged for his life and how he made him leave with not a stitch of clothing on. He got the last laugh, but that didn't stop Cindy. She was soon on to her next out-of-work, broke-ass nigga. By this time, Nathan had given up on him and Cindy. That's when he decided to start screwing around too. But his went a little too far.

Nathan sure showed Cindy with his screwing around. His playing around got his play thing, Shayla Hampton, pregnant. We believe in his effort to mess with Cindy, he just grabbed the first young thing that gave him the attention. When Cindy heard rumors about Nathan going with some young girl half his age, she was floored. But when she found out that Shayla was pregnant, she was livid. Shayla was about twenty-two, dark with braids, mostly weave extending the length of her back. She was short with an hourglass shape. She had a cute baby face that made her look younger than she was.

Cindy called on her street sources to find out any and everything about the girl. The girl, according to Cindy, was some street whore that lived in the town where Cindy was principal. When her sources told her who she was, to add insult to injury, she knew Shayla and her family. So it was easy for her to keep tabs on the girl. This bothered Nathan. He didn't mean for it to go that far. He just wanted to give Cindy a taste of her own medicine. Even with all her faults, he loved her, and he never meant to hurt her.

The night the girl went to the hospital to have the baby, one of Cindy's friends, Sharon, who was a nurse at the hospital called her and told her to come right then if she wanted to see the baby. Sharon slipped her into the maternity ward to see Nathan and Shayla's baby. Cindy broke down and cried because the baby was a splitting image of Nathan and their daughter, Sam. After that, they tried to keep their marriage afloat, but it was doomed because there was no trust between them anymore. So they divorced but became and remained good friends until Cindy's death.

The divorce, along with all the other drama, didn't change Cindy one iota. Instead of learning from her mistakes, she threw caution and evidently her senses in the gutter or somewhere because she sure didn't use her head. She became a loose woman in every sense of the word.

Cindy "left" her job as principal and applied for and got a job in St. Paul at the local community college. We think she got it because of Nathan pulling a few strings. Anyway, she was hired as a counselor where I was working as the outreach program coordinator. I forgot how we met to begin this amazing journey of friendship that forged a bond that I would never forget. We did almost everything together. I was the yin to her yang. She was the strong vocal one, and I was the organizer and the doer. It was always strange that we never just hung out on the weekends. There were times when we would do some things together but not often. Basically she did her thing, and I did mine. We would stay on the phone hours on end talking about any and everything and any and everybody. She gave me the strength to conquer that which needed changing in my life, and I gave her the support she needed to face her inner demons.

When a former girlfriend of my husband moved back to town and found out that he was married, she tried every trick in the book to come between us. It was Cindy that gave me the strength to fight back. "Never let any woman think that she has that much power over you," she said. "You show her that you will stand your ground and not back down." She really helped me through some trying times. My husband and his family were afraid of Ann Fleming and her mother because they were known as the local "root doctors." My husband, Chris, his family, and the community that Ann and her mother lived in believed in "root." I didn't and neither did my family. I was always told that the only way those kinds of people could hurt you was through your food or beverage. He tried to get his family to talk to her, but that was in vain. So they tried talking to me. "Just ignore her, and she'll stop," Chris's mother said. "Just don't make her mad."

Ann said that Chris had promised to marry her and that he was going to do it or else! Ann was a force to be reckoned with, but I was not going to back down. She found out where we lived and would drive up and down our street, blowing the horn and throwing trash in the yard. Then she got our number from a mutual friend that we both knew; and she would call the house and hang up, call and hang up, never saying anything. Eventually she figured the hang ups weren't getting anyplace. So she would call and curse me out, saying all sorts of ugly and nasty things. Enough was enough, so I reported her to the phone company and the sheriff's office. In the meantime, she was giving her other men and Chris clothes that she would steal from her job. He would just throw them in the trash, but I held on to a few things. She would leave them in the mailbox, in his car, and once she got so bold as to leave them on our step. She stopped for a while when Chris and his brothers threatened her. I told Cindy what was going on and how everybody was afraid of her, especially the men, because they felt that she would do something to them. I found out that this wasn't the first time that Ann had done something like this. When she was younger, a young minister came to preach at her church. She wanted him and did everything in her power to get him. She disrespected his wife and children and pursued him relentlessly. Finally he was weak and gave in and began sleeping with her. Well, she got pregnant by the minister; and when he wouldn't leave his wife for her, she tried to blackmail him into leaving. She would take the child to church and have her run up to him after church, yelling "daddy, daddy," knowing that his wife, children, and the members of the church would be standing there, talking with them. He would be so humiliated because he could not stand to see the hurt on his wife's face. The minister, not being able to deal with it any longer, went to the deacon board and confessed. They already knew the story of the affair, plus they knew Ann and her shadiness. When the deacons found out that she was blackmailing him, they kicked her out of the church. Eventually the pastor and his family moved to parts unknown and were never heard from again. That sent Ann on a revenge frenzy, and no man was safe. After the minister and his family left, she moved on to her next victim.

This guy, John Major, she told everybody that she was involved with him with heard the talk around town about her and decided that he didn't need this type of woman in his life. He stopped hanging out with her and started seeing someone. He told her that he really appreciated the help that she gave him when he first came to town. But he thinks that he needs to stop depending on her so much and start doing more for himself, but they will always be friends. It was just a chance meeting between the two of them. He was new to the area and didn't know anyone. He met her at the gas station. They struck up a conversation, and she gave him some helpful information. They would call each other from time to time, and she would have him over for dinner. In her mind, this meant that they were dating. So why did he say that they were just friends? A few months later, the guy, John, got hurt on the job and had to be hospitalized. While he was there, Ann went to visit him; and until this day, no one knows what happened to him. But he was never the same after her visit. His family had to put him in a mental institution. Well, this didn't scare me because, as I stated before, they can only harm you through food or drink, and I knew that I wasn't going to be around her like that. On the other hand, Chris and his family let this validate their beliefs. In a way, I felt sorry for Ann because she wanted so bad to be loved, but she went about it the wrong way. Oh well, you have to live and learn.

Cindy told me to call her job and tell them about the clothes that she was stealing and giving Chris. I did, and sure enough they had suspected that she had been stealing but couldn't prove it. When I called and told them that I had pants, shirts, and underwear with their facility's name in them, they sent security down to pick them up that Tuesday. They watched her for a week, and sure enough they had what they needed to call her in. That next Tuesday, they called her to the office with the evidence and fired her on the spot. She cussed, fussed, and threatened me for days, but I didn't care because she was out of my hair. As Cindy said, "One battle won." Even though she lost her job, we had a good laugh about the lengths she would go to get a man, good old Ann. We just didn't understand it. Ann was a weird-looking character, and no one understood how she got all those men. But like I said, they were afraid of her, and a lot of times we think that she mistook their kindness for having feelings for her. But then again, as we women know, "Men are weak-minded and think with their second head." Eventually she became a thing of the past and moved out of town. No one knew where she went, and I really don't think anyone cared. Anyway, Cindy got me through that drama.

Chapter 3

Friendship

Cindy was always the talk of the town. She was an educated and well-versed individual; but just to look at and talk to her, you wouldn't know it. She was plenty "ghetto fab" and then some. At first, I don't think either one of us knew how to take the other. In the beginning, we were cordial with each other, making small talk at meetings and such. Then at a meeting we both attended, we were asked to visit one of the neighboring community colleges to observe a program that we were trying to implement at our school. So it was on this trip to a college in Landon, South Carolina, that we started talking and found out that we had a lot in common, even down to our parents knowing each other. A friendship was forged, one that would stand the test of time and tribulations. We became fast and inseparable BFFs. Her mother was glad of the friendship, and later she would tell me that I was the only true friend that Cindy had.

Cindy was godsend. I finally had someone that I could talk to about anything and knew that it would stay between the two of us. We had each other's back through thick and thin, right or wrong. When you saw one, you knew that the other one was not far behind. They knew that Cindy was the vocal one and didn't mind telling you how she felt about anything, including you. For the most part, they would leave us alone because we could stand on our own, by our self, but together we were a force that no one wanted to deal with. It had gotten to the point that one day, we were arguing in the hall about something, and the president of the college was coming toward us. He stopped and looked puzzled at us. He said, "What in the world? You two are arguing!" We had to laugh at that ourselves. Everybody knew how close we were.

At the beginning of the school year in August, Cindy began a new relationship with a church member of hers who just happened to be my cousin, Robert Johnson. Well, Robert was supposed to be God's gift to women. Joyce and I could not figure out for the life of us what these women saw in Robert. He was about five eleven, on the thick side, more muscle thick than fat thick. He was a local "bouncer" for clubs, parties, etc. which we figured was what made him attractive to the women. That and he must have had gold hanging off his you know what. "Ain't no way in the world." We would laugh. It had to be dripping with gold! Whatever Joyce and I were missing, the other women must have seen it because they would lose their freaking minds over him. But he also had a live-in baby momma. Janice was younger than Robert, a basic country girl who worshipped the grounds that he walked on. Like all the other fellas in town, Robert had heard the rumors about Cindy and sleeping with any and everybody, so it was only natural that he would try to dip into the honey pot. Now, he was younger than Cindy, but he knew from the talk around town that age didn't matter to her if they were over eighteen. So he pursued her.

Their romance began with them working on the same committees at church. They would have to see each other at least once a week after church for brief meetings. Then they were elected to cochair a project which meant that they needed to meet at other times outside of the church setting. At first, it was after hours at church. Then it was at one of the local restaurants, then innocent meetings at her house. Since this was a small town, it wasn't much you could hide from the prying eyes of nosy people. Day meetings turned into evening meetings, then night meetings and, before long, overnight meetings. Cindy would often come to work and talk about her night with Robert. She would show me the rug burns on her knees from her lovemaking sessions with him. Then she would look at me laughing and say, "Brett, you and Chris with his bougie ass should try it. You might like it!" I looked at her and gave her the middle finger. She would then say, "Tell Chris to keep wishing it'll grow!" Then we both would burst out laughing.

The buzz was on, and again Cindy was thrusted into the limelight. I think Robert forgot about Janice and their two children which he had living in a broken-down trailer on the edge of town next to an old car junkyard. Cindy would see Janice speak and smile like nothing was going on, thinking that she was none the wiser. Janice suspected something but couldn't believe the rumors because Miss Cindy always treated her nice. Cindy said that she was in love with Robert, but I knew better. Robert, knowing that he had responsibilities with Janice, had feelings for both women. Cindy and Robert got bolder and bolder with their newfound love and were even taking weekend trips out of town, leaving Janice at home to take care of the children. Things were beginning to get messy! One night, when Cindy and Robert were settling in at her house in front of the fireplace, watching TV in the den, there was this loud crash, followed by the sound of shattering glass. They rushed to the living room in time to see Cindy's paned glass windows shattering over her living room floor. "What the hell is going on?" she shouted.

Janice was in the yard, crying and yelling at the top of her voice, "Robert! Robert! I love you! Don't do this to our family! Please come home. We need you. Robert, don't do this to us!"

Lights were going on at the surrounding houses in the neighborhood. Curtains were being pushed back, and doors being cracked so that they wouldn't miss this. Still pleading and begging, Janice fell to her knees. "Robert! Please, please, please! Don't do this to us." Ashamed and upset, Robert went outside to comfort her. He calmed her down enough and took her home. He stayed with her until she fell asleep but goes right back to Cindy's.

Cindy was still visibly upset and cussing up a storm. "What the fuck is wrong with that crazy bitch? I am going to have her arrested and sue the shit out of her!" Robert knew that it was no need in trying to talk to her while she was in that frame of mind, so he went home to Janice and his children.

The next day, true to her word, she filed a report with the police department. Her ex-husband, Nathan, heard about what happened and talked with her, asking her to think about it for a day or two. He knew Janice and knew that this was out of character for her. "Hell no," Cindy replied. "'I want that bitch in jail." Nathan told Cindy that he understood but felt that she still needed to think about it. In the meantime, Robert, feeling guilty and not wanting the mother of his children in jail, tried talking to Cindy, but that was a short-lived conversation that went in one ear and out the other. Losing all hope, Robert decided to go and talk to Cindy's parents. He laid out the whole scenario of what had been going on which her parents had heard of and were not surprised. They told him that they did not go along with what he and Cindy were doing. They also didn't agree with the fact that even though Janice was wrong for breaking out the windows, she was a victim in all of this and did not deserve to go to jail. So they told him that they would talk with Cindy about not pressing charges if he and Janice agreed to replace the windows. They also told Robert that he should stop seeing their daughter and try to be there for Janice and his children. So Cindy's parents talked to her and explained to her that they didn't want another scandal linked to her and that this wouldn't have happened if she hadn't been going with Robert. She agreed not to file charges and gave Janice two weeks to replace the windows. Cindy's parents also told her that she should consider leaving Robert alone because in the eyes of the law, they are common-law husband and wife, also think about the children. That only added fuel to the fire and made Cindy want Robert even more not because she loved him but because he had become forbidden. Cindy's going to show Janice who ruled the roost and turned up the fire. First, she tried to monopolize all of Robert's time. This was getting to be too much for Janice to handle, so she went to talk with Cindy's parents and apologized for what she had done. She also asked them if they would talk to Cindy and ask her to stop seeing Robert. She told them that he and the children were all that she had. Their hearts went out to her. Janice McMillan looked to be a mare child herself, and that was because she was only nineteen. She was of medium height, dark with a childlike cuteness about her. She had a nice talk with Cindy's parents, Mr. and Mrs. Smalls, and told them that she was going to talk to the minister.

Janice called and made an appointment to meet with the minister. She met with Reverend Cave the following Wednesday and told him what was going on with her, Robert, and Cindy. She told him about breaking out the windows and said that she knew that she was wrong; but at the time, she was trying to get Robert's attention. Reverend Cave said that he would speak with Cindy and Robert; but before he could, Janice confronted Cindy after service one Sunday in church. This was not the thing to do to Cindy, make her feel that she has been backed into a corner. She was fighting mad, and poor Janice was just stupid to confront Cindy in this manner and in all places the church. This was not the place or time to air dirty laundry. But they went at it nonetheless. Cindy went to walk away, and Janice made the mistake of grabbing her arm to stop her. All hell broke loose then! Cindy, forgetting where she was, and started cussing like a sailor. Janice, by this time, was beginning to back down, but it was a little too late. Reverend Cave stepped in and intervened, "Ladies, remember where you are," he warned. Cindy got it together and apologized to Reverend Cave for her behavior and for cursing in the church of all places. So after that, Cindy stopped seeing Robert for a while, but Cindy is the type who wants what she can't or shouldn't have, and she was a firm believer in payback. So it wasn't long before she started seeing Robert again. By now, Robert and Janice had gotten married but what did Cindy care. She was going to get the bitch back come hell or high water. To Cindy, this was an even greater challenge, one that she was gladly accepting. When the town got wind of them sneaking around again, word quickly got back to his wife. This time, in a desperate move, Janice shot herself and where was Robert? You guessed it, at Cindy's. One of Robert's brothers came to get him so that he could go to the hospital. He got there just in time to ride with her to Hillsborough, North Carolina. According to Cindy, the bitch shot herself in the "pussy." She wasn't trying to kill herself. She was just trying to get Robert's attention again, Cindy's words, not mine. They had to medevac her to a hospital in Hillsborough because of where the bullet lodged. Now everybody was upset and blamed Cindy for

Janice trying to kill herself. She was the outcast of St. Paul; and everyone rallied against her in favor of Janice, even Robert's favorite aunt, Shirley Carter, who thought the world of Cindy. Conversations that Cindy would have with people on the streets quickly turned into polite hellos and fast retreats before a conversation could start. They were calling her bitch, whore, and home-wrecker. This did not phase Cindy one bit. One day in passing, a woman called her a bitch. She looked at the woman and said, "That's Miss Bitch to you because I'm a certified card carrying one because I'm excellent at what I do!"

Then she looked at me and said, "Brett, I don't know if these people realize it or not, but it takes a lot to embarrass me. So I hope that these simple ass bitches know that they are not hurting me one bit. If they keep fucking with me, I'll show them and fuck their man." So life went on for her, and she was moving on to her next fella.

This time, Cindy completely lost all her senses and started dating this eighteen-year-old drug dealer, Warren Butler. He was stunning and looked like he could have been a male model. Well, Cindy tried to keep this relationship under wraps, but it was getting harder and harder. Warren wanted the world to know that he was sleeping with a college teacher, as he put it. Boy, oh boy, the stories she would tell us about her and Warren's lovemaking made me and Joyce want to go and get us an eighteen-year-old. I mean, her accounts kept us on the edge of our seats. She had us laughing until we cried.

One day, Cindy came to work barely able to walk, "What's wrong with you?" I asked.

"Girl, Warren put me through the wringer last night, legs over the shoulders, one leg here while the other one is over there. He had me on my head, on my knees, every which way you could think of. One time, I thought that I was a wishbone." No explanation needed. She laughed. "That young stud had me coming like a twenty-year-old. I 'bout lost my mind up in there! I sure slept good last night."

"Yeah, I'm sure you did," I said.

Joyce, not to be outdone, said, "But whose old ass can barely walk today?"

"That's all right, bitch." Cindy smirked. "And it was sure damn worth it!"

That relationship was short-lived because Warren had his drug contact to send him drugs through the mail. When he went to pick up the package from the post office, the Feds were waiting for him. Cindy always said, "He wasn't the brightest bulb on the Christmas tree. But boy, could he fuck!"

"Shut your mouth!" Joyce and I said in unison.

"But I'm talking about Warren!" The three of us fell out laughing.

Chapter 4

Lenell

I forgot where and when Cindy met Lenell Wright. Talk about a big-time country boy from the sticks. This was the poster boy. I'm pretty sure he is one of the guys on the commercial for FarmersOnly.com. He was as sweet as could be; he was a hard worker and must have saved every penny he made. So he had a little bit of money, and that's all Cindy needed to know. Cindy couldn't wait to get her hands on his money. It didn't take long for her to have him under her spell. He was separated from his common-law wife and children. These were older children, and they thought it was great that their dad was dating a teacher. They seemed happy together, and he did everything possible to keep Cindy that way. My husband and I would visit sometimes, and we even went out once or twice together. Cindy told me that she was content which I thought was wonderful. During the time they were dating, Lenell bought her a car since she was having so many problems with hers. You should have seen Cindy cruising around town in that spanking brand-new candy apple red Camaro. It was a nice car. This kept her grounded for a while, and she devoted all her attention to Lenell.

Lenell would tell his family and friends just how lucky he was to have Cindy in his life. Only thing that was wrong, Cindy could not cook. I mean Cindy couldn't boil an egg without burning it. All was not lost since Lenell loved to cook, so this wasn't a problem. "Wright," she would say, "I don't know what we're going to eat tonight."

"Don't worry, baby. I gotcha," he would say. That's all she wanted to hear. This relationship went on for a few years. We all thought that he was the one. Boy, were we wrong! None of us ever suspected that she was secretly seeing someone else. Brad Wilson, the new "side" guy, was from my old stomping ground, Cedartown, a quaint little town nestled in the foothills of North Carolina near Laurens, North Carolina. We found out because she needed us to cover for her. Yeah, we were the fools always coming to her aid. Good or bad, one of us was always there. She had to let us in on it because he was meeting her down the street from Lenell's house at her cousin Shelia's apartment. Cindy and Sheila were tight as thieves and always had each other's backs because they grew up together and were more like sisters than cousins. Sheila was a "druggie," and everybody knew this about her. Sheila was a survivor and would do whatever it took to get what she needed. Shelia was high one night and wandered into the wrong place at the wrong time and got in the midst of a brutal fight, resulting in her almost losing her life. She survived but lost her arm in the process. She was a stay-at-home mom with two girls. The oldest, Mary, finished high school last year and had a job at one of the local restaurants. Janie is a senior in high school and hopes to graduate this year. Sheila doesn't have anyone to really take care of except herself because the girls can fend for themselves, plus most of their time is spent at their grandmother's house. So Sheila gets fucked up and has parties at her place whenever she feels the need which is all the time. She's loyal if you meet her demands of booze and drugs. To keep her secret, Cindy would give her a couple of dollars here and there to help with the cause. Well, this night, Cindy must have come up short because Sheila wasn't hearing about Brad meeting Cindy at her house and threatened to tell Lenell if she didn't give her a little something, something to fill her needs. Between Brad and Cindy, they came up with enough to get her a hit. "This it?" she whined. Wanting more and not being able to get it, this didn't sit too good with Sheila. The next day, she went full steam to Lenell and told him everything. She told him how Cindy was going out with this fellow from Cedartown and that he ran a club down there. Knowing Sheila, Lenell half-believed what she was telling him. He listened, but he had to find this out for himself.

Brad Wilson wasn't married but was living with his girlfriend, Wanda, and together they had two children. Brad had been married and, as a matter of fact, lived down the street from his ex-wife and son. He was willing to leave Wanda for Cindy but realized how much this would hurt her, and he couldn't do it. He stayed with Wanda and still saw Cindy on the side. After Lenell did some investigating and found out that Sheila was telling the truth about Cindy's cheating, he played it cool. He even went to the club where Brad worked a couple of times and hung out. He didn't say a thing to Cindy and went about as if everything was just fine. In the meantime, he started following her until he saw and got enough evidence.

One night, Cindy had been to see Brad and was on her way home. She pulled up into the driveway, stopped, and got out of the car. As she unlocked and opened the front door to go in, she felt this great force shove her into the living room. She fell hard on the floor. Before she could get to her feet, she felt her hair being grabbed and pulled as if it was coming out of the scalp. Weave was flying all over the place. Finally, Lenell began to talk, "You no good FUCKING BITCH! DID YOU THINK THAT YOU COULD CHEAT ON ME AND I WOULDN'T FIND OUT?" He beat her up pretty bad that night before leaving her on the floor with a swollen and bloody face, bald spots in her head, and numerous bruises over the rest of her body, and he took the keys to his car. No one saw Cindy for a couple of days. It was if she just disappeared from the face of the earth. Since Lenell took the car, no one knew that she was at home. Bits and pieces of what happened that night slowly began to surface. I called Cindy and went to her house, but she would not answer the phone or come to the door. It got to a point where her mother was calling me, trying to find out what was going on. I told her that I didn't know and had only heard "street talk." I told her what I heard that was being said about Lenell beating Cindy up but that I hadn't seen or talked to Cindy in a few days. She won't answer the phone or come to the door when I called or would go around there. Hearing this, Mrs. Smalls went to her house and made her open the door. Mrs. Smalls almost fainted at the sight of Cindy. She took her immediately to the doctor. It was bad. The doctor said that in addition to the swollen face and bruises, she had a broken rib and a sprained wrist and ankle. She also had minor scrapes and bruises on her knees. He gave her something for the pain and to help her rest, and then he told her to stay in bed for the rest of the week. He told her that if she had any problems, give him a call. Cindy's mother was furious and wanted to press charges against Lenell, but Cindy didn't want or need the attention and begged her not to. When she began to feel better, she pleaded with Lenell to forgive her and take her back. It was a done deal, and all the crying and begging she did fell on deaf ears. Lenell was through, and nothing Cindy could say or do would change his mind. Cindy admitted defeat, stayed out of sight for a while, and almost lost her job because she stopped going to work. Her next victim, um, I mean man was a piece of work.

Chapter 5

Are You Kidding Me?

Cindy went a little too far out left field this time. She started staying in the country with some man that she met at a club. His name was James Moody, and he had just been released from jail for who knows what. He was a halfway decent-looking man with muscles. I guess from working out in jail. He stayed so far in the country that I know the sunshine had to be pumped in. After doing some inquiring, we found out that Cindy was staying in the country with James. "Why?" is still a mystery to us. We had no idea where he lived, so we asked around town and finally got directions to his trailer. We drove out there Friday after work. Lord, it was so far in the woods that we got turned around and lost a couple of times. Thank the Lord we finally found the place. He lived in a single wide trailer that had seen better days. As we pulled into the yard, chickens, pigs, and goats scattered and ran everywhere. We honked the horn because neither me nor Joyce was getting out. After the second honk, a young boy came to the door. I spoke and told him that we were looking for a James Moody. He said, "That's my uncle." I asked if he was home. He said yes.

"Could you ask him to come to the door?" With what seemed like forever, he finally came to the door with a nasty attitude.

"What you want with me?" he yelled.

"We're looking for Cindy Porter," I responded.

"Who you?" he asked.

"I'm Brett, and this is Joyce. We are friends of Cindy. Have you seen her?" I asked.

"Yeah, she here. Get out and come in," he said. The things we did for Cindy, against our better judgment we got out and walked up some shaky steps to get in the trailer. The smell of urine and some other sickening foul odor met us at the door. It was so strong that we almost gagged. He led us to a back room where Cindy was asleep on the bottom bunk bed. On the top bunk was another man whom we later found out was James's brother whom he shared the room with. In addition to the two of them, James's mother, sister, and nephew lived in the trailer too. Anyway, Cindy was sleeping on the bottom bunk that she shared with James. My eyes welled up with tears when I saw the conditions she had stooped to. I shook her and called her name a few times. She woke up and looked around as if she was trying to figure out where she was. She looked at me and Joyce and called our names. Then she jumped up, hugged us, and started crying. Boy, did she smell awful! The urine odor that met us at the door was in her clothes and on her skin. We suspected that Cindy had a problem; but after seeing her here, in our minds, it was confirmed. We needed to get her some help and fast. After much pleading, we got her to leave with us. Cindy was a mental mess! Lenell really did a number on her. We took her to her mother's house where she stayed for a couple of weeks. Her mother and I encouraged her to take a week off from work. I would stop by after work to check on her, and she seemed to be on the mend. One day, when I stopped by, I was greeted by the old Cindy that I knew and loved. We talked a long time about Lenell and how she thought that she really loved him, but she just couldn't help herself when she cheated on him. I asked her if she thought that she might be afraid of commitment. She said that she felt that it had a lot to do with it. "Anyway," she said, "That's water under the bridge."

Well, for some reason, she couldn't help herself; and during the summer, she kept seeing James. It was a summer romance. At least that's what we thought. It's a good thing that we didn't bet the farm on it. They became hooked at the hip. When you saw one, you saw the other. Her parents, especially her mother, didn't care for him at all. He was loud, ill-mannered, and grungy-looking, an all-around ghetto nigga. Joyce and I couldn't stand him either, but we put up with him because of Cindy. When we would ask her why James. She would simply say, "Something to do." This lasted until December, until his baby mama drama came a-knockin' and brought her live-in woman with her. She told James that she was tired of his sorry ass, and it was time he gave her some money for his son. And if he didn't start giving her money every week like he said he was, she was taking him to family court. *Family court*, two words no man wanted to hear. He tried to explain to her that he was between jobs, but she knew that he was getting an unemployment check. So things were starting to get loud and ugly. She told him that she bet he was spending all his money on his college teacher bitch. By this time, she was wagging her finger in his face. Sara must have gotten a little too close for comfort because he pushed her hand away from him, big mistake! Sara's woman, Rhonda, leaped on him and told him not to ever touch her woman again! Now, Rhonda was average height with the prettiest wavy black hair. She had out grown her female features and looked, talked, and acted like a male. She was straight-up Butch. I met Rhonda a while ago when I taught her former girlfriend's daughter in one of our summer programs. She would come to all the activities with her, and I found her to be quite likeable. You could tell that Rhonda was interested in the well-being of Lillie's daughter.

Back to the fight. They were punching, shoving, and rolling in the street. That "woman" pistol whipped James from one end of the street to the other. They had to call the cops to get her off him; and believe me, he was fighting her like a man. We can laugh about it now; but at the time, we were either too shocked or too scared to make a sound. But we did some running! Remember the cartoons from back in the day and how the legs looked when they were running? Their legs were spinning around and around at top speed. Well, I think that we gave them a run for their money because Joyce, Cindy, and I did some moving that day. None of us knew that we could run that fast.

Cindy lay low for a while and concentrated on herself for a change. She spent a week with Sam during the Christmas holidays.

Then she stayed with me and Chris for a couple of days when she got back. We had a blast! Joyce came over and spent a night, so we had a girl's night. I don't think we ever went to sleep. The next day, we jumped in the car and went shopping. But Cindy was getting that look in her eyes, and we knew what that meant, "need a man!" Again, she set her sights on Robert; but this time, he was not available, at least not for her.

Chapter 6

The Tangled Web

Robert and Janice moved on from each other. They divorced, and Janice did something that she should have done a long time ago. She grew up, stopped depending on Robert, and started thinking for herself. She made a clean break from him, went back to school, got her GED, went on to college, and got her degree in engineering. She now leads one of the departments at one of the top engineering firms in the state of NC. The job sends her all over the world, representing them. The kids are doing great and have both earned degrees from four-year colleges. Robert, on the other hand, is doing what he does best, getting by on someone else's dime. He has no place of his own and was staying with his mother until he decided to give his "favorite" aunt a surprise birthday party and not invite his mother who just happens to be his favorite aunt's sister. The irony of it is he was staying with his mother scotch free, not giving her one red cent to help with expenses. His mother, Dell, even paid his car insurance. He would go around telling people that Dell didn't do nuthin' for him, that his mother was just no good. Now, Dell had been married and was together with her husband until his unexpected death. All her children were by her husband. On the other hand, her sister had never been married, had three children by three different men, and never heard from them. Oh, but how Robert worshipped the ground his Aunt Shirley walked on. This lasted for a couple of years until one day when the shit hit the fan. Shirley worked for the

Baxters, one of the wealthiest white families in St. Paul, and this made her feel that she was a privileged black woman 'cause Boss Man and Boss Lady sure is good to her. She lived in a modest house on the other side of town; she had a piece of a car to get her back and forth to work and around town. Nonetheless, yes siree bob, according to her, the Baxters treated her good.

Her son, Jason Carter, rented an old run-down building of the Baxters in the back lot in St. Paul and opened a barbeque place. They were open Wednesdays through Saturdays. It must have had about fifty employees. Everybody, their cousin, uncle, and brother worked there. They had more employees than customers and food to cook. But those employees showed up for work every day. Rumors started to circulate that it was a front for drugs. So the cops began watching the place. Somebody said that they planted an undercover guy back there to keep an eye on things. A lot of good that did when one of their friends was a deputy sheriff and kept them abreast of what was going on. Soon the BBQ joint was the hangout place. Before long, they opened a hair and nail salon. The Carters looked to be unstoppable. Everybody wanted to be their friend. Things got kind of rocky for a minute. Someone spilled the beans about their friend being a deputy sheriff. Law enforcement agents started feeding him false information; so when they made the bust, he was caught up in the middle. The deputy went to jail, and the Carters lost almost everything and had to file bankruptcy. They didn't stay down forever. It took them about two years to make a comeback. This time, they rebuilt the BBQ joint bigger and better than ever. Boy, did they ever put their ass on their shoulders then! You couldn't tell them anything. They were the "big niggas" in St. Paul. Unbeknownst to the people of St. Paul, the BBQ place was owned by a silent partner, a foreigner, who was using them to sell his drugs and launder money in exchange for the use of the buildings that he built for them. Well, this bit of information was kept from Shirley. She thought that her son was running a legit business; and Robert, even though it had never been discussed, thought that he had a share in business with Jason since they were so close and did everything together. Was he ever wrong and he was about to get schooled.

Since Robert was telling everybody about their "business" and bragging about what they had, his mom, Dell Johnson, felt that she could go to the shop and help. When she was asked to leave, she wanted to know why she had to leave when her son was part owner. That's when the shit hit the fan! "Part owner, part owner of what?" asked Shirley. Dell, not knowing what was going on, continued defending her son. This sent Shirley into a tailspin. "Robert, don't own shit around here. He is a hired hand just like everybody else." Hitting her chest, she said, "All of this belongs to my son." Robert, who was standing in back making sauce, heard the commotion and rushed out front. Shirley made sure that he understood exactly what his job was because she repeated it several times. You could see the hurt on his face. Well, things kind of cooled down between Robert and his favorite aunt, Shirley. But through all of this, Dell was still there in his corner, encouraging and supporting him.

Chapter 7

Brenda

By this time, Robert and Cindy had renewed their friendship, but he had moved on to a new love interest, a faculty member from Dale University, one of the local colleges in the area. Brenda Howard had recently moved here from Alabama, a young naive girl with no idea about what she was fixing to get tangled up in. She had been trying to meet Robert for some time now. In talking with Carol Ott, a friend of hers that worked at Dale with her, she found out that her and Robert had been friends forever. Bingo! That was Brenda's way in. Carol arranged a meeting between Brenda and Robert, and Brenda fell head over heels in love with him on the spot. Girls beware, Brenda had marked him as hers, and no one else could have him. Brenda became obsessed with Robert and followed him everywhere he worked.

In one of his many talks with Cindy, he told her about Brenda and said that he wanted Cindy to meet Brenda. He took her to meet Cindy, and they hit it off almost instantly. As Cindy and Brenda got to know each other, Brenda began to look at Cindy as an older sister, someone she could talk to, especially what was going on with her and Robert. During the time that Brenda was confining in Cindy, Robert and Cindy were on the verge of renewing their romance. This was a little secret that they kept from Brenda. They would meet late at night at Cindy's house, out of town, at "out of the way" places, or even at Robert's mother's house. Poor Brenda was none the wiser. If she didn't hear from or see Robert, she went crying on Cindy's shoulder. Cindy in return would play the ever-so-concerned friend, all the time wanting her to leave so that she could go jump in the sack with Robert. Joyce and I told her that she was wrong and needed to stop seeing Robert or stop being Brenda's go-to girl. Cindy didn't listen and got involved deeper and deeper in Brenda and Robert's life. The next year, Brenda was pregnant for Robert, but this didn't stop Cindy and Robert. Well, for one thing, he was an old no good dog. Joyce and I figured at this point that Cindy just liked the idea of the game.

It really began to irk me and Joyce when they started using Brenda. Cindy saw nothing wrong with it. Brenda started going to Robert and Cindy's church where she would later become a member. Brenda became very active in the church and began working on some of the same committees as Robert and Cindy. The church and its members welcomed Brenda with open arms.

The church decided to do a calendar for Mother's Day, honoring mothers in the church and around the community. Since Brenda did this kind of work, they asked her if she would spearhead it. She gladly accepted and worked closely with Robert and Cindy to make the calendar. Brenda did an outstanding job; but when it was time to pay for the work, the calendar cost more to make than they anticipated because the church kept changing things. The members made a big fuss over it and refused to pay her the extra money. Rather than sink to their level and since it was for the church, Brenda took the loss which was close to a thousand dollars. Cindy and Robert called her stupid, laughed about it, and said that it was a lesson learned. Still, Brenda was none the wiser. Was she one of those dumb blonds? Joyce and I didn't agree with Cindy on the way that they treated her and didn't see anything humorous about the whole thing. This was one of those times that I was sorry that Cindy was my friend. There were moments when I felt like telling Brenda just what was going on but why open up a can of whip ass.

Chapter 8

RJ

That July, Brenda had a baby boy and named him Robert Jr. whom they called RJ for short. Brenda asked Cindy to be the godmother which she happily accepted. Cindy played the honored godmother to the tee. She would buy gifts for RJ and babysit him so that Robert and Brenda could have "alone time." On the other hand, naming him after Robert was the worst thing Brenda could have done. This opened the flood gates of hell and all of Robert's baby mamas came out of every whorehouse, cotton field, outhouse, and wormhole you could think of. In addition to Cindy and Brenda, Robert was seeing about four other women. Two had babies for him. One was pregnant, and the other had her baby within days of Brenda giving birth. What's the first thing they cried? Child support!

It was a time none of them knew about the other; and to make matters even *worse*, Robert's mother knew about all of them and was seeing them on a regular basis. Since all of them wanted Robert, what better way to win him over than by going out of their way to be nice to the mother? They did everything for Dell except wipe her butt, and they would have done that too if she asked them to. Dell would be dressed from head to toe in her matching outfits that her "daughters-in-law" bought her. She milked it for all it was worth, knowing that none of them suspected that she knew about Brenda. So when the shit hit the fan, she had to hurry and do damage control. She was devastated to know that Robert was going with this Brenda. This is the lie she told them when they approached her to confirm the news. "Baby, I was just as shocked as you when I heard about it!" she lied. Now Dell's favorite baby mama, Betty, knew Dell and knew that that was a bunch of bull. Dell didn't have any dealings with Brenda because early in the relationship, Robert told Brenda not to fall into his mother's trap and let her use her into buying her things and giving her money. When she didn't do that, it just put a bad taste in Dell's mouth, and she couldn't stand her! Betty quickly let her presence be known since Robert was still coming to her house, and she had a ten-year-old daughter for him. Betty did everything for Robert and his mother. She knew about Brenda and Cindy, but she didn't care because it was understood that he was going to marry her.

Evidently Brenda didn't get the memo because she knew for a fact that he was marrying her. This was just too much for Brenda to handle, so off to her mother's house in Alabama she went, with RJ in tow. For a while, no one knew where she was. I think Robert and Cindy knew but didn't care at the time. Robert felt that Brenda needed time to cool down, plus it gave Robert much needed alone time with Cindy without Brenda breathing down their necks. Finally after about a week or so, Robert went to get Brenda and RJ. He had never been to her home in Alabama but had spoken to her mother many times. Therefore, he had no problem going down there. Little did he know what was waiting for him when he got there.

Chapter 9

Surprise!

It was late at night when Robert got to Logan; but since they were expecting him, Brenda and her mother were still up. Brenda's mother's house was on the outskirts of town surrounded by lots of trees. It was a nice modest house painted white with blue trim. As Robert walked cautiously down the sidewalk, making sure he wasn't stepping on a snake or any other creature, he reached the steps and crept up them because of all the flowers. Reaching the porch, he knocked on the door, and the porch light immediately came on. "Who is it?" a voice called out from inside.

"It's me, Robert," he answered. Brenda's mother opened the door and invited him in. Brenda will be right out. She just went to check on the baby. After the niceties and such, the three of them talked for a short while until Brenda's mother excused herself. Brenda and Robert stayed up most of the night, trying to hash out their problems. With the morning light brought new surprises. It seemed that Brenda had a few well-kept secrets of her own, two to be exact. Robert met Brenda's daughter and son. That's right. Brenda had two children that no one knew about in St. Paul. Brenda had pulled the wool over everyone's eyes, playing the innocent, sweet young country bumpkin from the sticks. This was just too much for Robert to handle, so he got in his car and left in shock and alone. The player got played. He left Brenda right where he found her and went home to St. Paul and straight to Betty. That night, he went to see Cindy and told her about his ordeal in Alabama. Cindy had suspected that Brenda had a child, but she never thought that there were two of them.

Brenda came back a couple of days after Robert's visit and went directly to Cindy, sitting on the couch, crying and snorting about how sorry she was for not being up-front and honest with them. Cindy told her that she was not the one that she should be explaining to. She asked Cindy if she would watch RJ while she went to find and talk to Robert.

Robert had taken the day off and was hanging out at one of the local car washes. Robert saw Brenda coming and tried to get away, but he wasn't quick enough. So he had to listen to her trying to explain everything to him. For the most part, I think it went in one ear and out the other. I won't say that he didn't care. I just think that he was more hurt than anything else. It wasn't the fact that she had children. It was the idea of her not being up-front about them. He told her that he needed a couple of days to think about everything and that he would be in touch. After talking with Cindy, he did give Brenda a call mainly because of RJ, and they picked up their relationship from where they left off.

Robert, Cindy, and Brenda were back in their love triangle, and Brenda was still none the wiser and continued crying on Cindy's shoulder and wanting to know why Robert treated her the way that he did. As stated before, he worked at the BBQ joint and, get this, lived out of the back of his truck. That's right. Robert, by any other standard, would be considered homeless. That's why we figured he must have had gold hanging off his you know what.

Time went by fast; and before we knew it, RJ was four and was beginning to notice things. We told Cindy to be careful with what she did or said around him, but she said that RJ wasn't that bright. Throughout life, you are going to find people like Cindy that think they know everything and can't be told anything. Little did she know that RJ was going to blow their relationship out of the water.

Chapter 10

Mrs. Smalls

As though all this mess with Brenda and Robert wasn't enough, in September shortly after Labor Day, Cindy and her family began to notice little changes in her mother, Mrs. Smalls. It wasn't until later that I would find out that her mother had mental issues. Anyway, she started losing weight, and her whole attitude changed. Gone was the sweet, kind, and understanding woman. Instead, she became judgmental with a nasty disposition, a mare shell of the woman she used to be. People outside of the family were noticing it also. People began talking, wondering, and speculating about what was going on. Close friends and family began to avoid her because of the sudden mood swings. Cindy, Samantha, and Mr. Smalls couldn't figure out what was wrong, so they took her to the family doctor.

They talked with him and told him what was worrying them about her and how her behavior had changed. After examining and talking with her, he recommended that they take her to a psychologist in Tennessee. He would have his nurse make the appointment.

Once arriving in Tennessee, they headed to Dr. Nimmons's office. Cindy spoke with Dr. Johnson first to voice their concerns. After talking with Cindy, the doctor spoke with Mrs. Smalls one-on-one. When he finished talking with Mrs. Smalls, he called Cindy, Mr. Smalls, and Sam back in to the office and had a nurse take Mrs. Smalls to another room. He told them what was going on with the mother. First, he asked them if they knew that she wasn't sleeping at night. She would sit up all night long, rocking in her chair. He also told them that the weight lost came from her not eating not because she was on a diet and therefore was the reason she had lost over sixty pounds. Since she had been a heavyset woman all her adult life, everybody just thought that she was dieting. The doctor said that Mrs. Smalls was in bad shape. It was a good thing that they got her to him when they did, any longer and it could have been too late. Dr. Nimmons wanted to commit her, but she was not hearing that. The family could have signed her in, but they felt that it would have done more harm than good, plus Mr. Smalls was not going to leave his wife there, crying and going on like she was.

In the weeks to follow, she was getting worse, and medicines Dr. Nimmons prescribed for her were not helping. Cindy believed that she wasn't swallowing the pills, so she tried putting them in applesauce and giving it to her. She ate some of the applesauce, but it wasn't enough to do any good. She would not go back to Dr. Nimmons and would not seek medical attention elsewhere. Then one day, her body couldn't take any more of the abuse, and she collapsed. Luckily it was at a time when Cindy was at the house. They called the ambulance, and they started CPR on her in route to the hospital. She was put on life support, but it was just too late. She died a few days later.

Mrs. Smalls was Cindy's world; and after her death, Cindy was never the same. Cindy blamed herself for not realizing just how sick she was. In talking, one day, she told me what happened leading up to her mother's death. I did my best to assure her that it was not her fault.

I was talking to my mother and telling her about what happened leading up to her death and how Cindy was blaming herself for her mother's death. That's when Momma said that Mrs. Smalls had been committed to a mental institute before.

Cindy didn't cope well with her mother's death at all. She went to pieces. She gave up on life. She was a mess and couldn't come back to work. It was almost two weeks before she came back to work, but she was still a mess. She cried most of the day and couldn't get any work done. Students were beginning to complain about her never being in her office. They were upset because they didn't understand what was going on. Faculty, staff, and the president tried to be understanding, but they also needed her there to do her job. A friend of Cindy's, Pat, volunteered to come in and help her. This made a big difference. Between the two of us, we were able to help the students and catch up the majority of her paperwork.

This day, Pat had a doctor's appointment and could not come in. I went to her room to check on her and found her crying uncontrollably. It was a good thing that there weren't any students in there. I tried to calm her down, but nothing I said or did worked. So I told her to go home, and I would take over her afternoon counseling session. I called my office and told my secretary where I was and to hold down the fort until I returned. I told Cindy that I would stop by to check on her on my way home.

On my way home, I swung by to see how she was doing and if she needed anything before I left. She just needed to talk. She told me that she was bipolar and had panic attacks. For some reason, this didn't surprise me because Joyce and I knew that something was wrong, but we just couldn't put our finger on it. She said that she was taking medicines to help control them, but she didn't like the way they made her feel. She said what really scared her was that she didn't want to end up like her mother. I told her that I would be there to help her stay on top of her illness and remind her to take her "crazy pills" as she called them.

Cindy started coming to work late, or she wouldn't show up for work at all. She would not call the office to let them know whether she was coming or if she would be late. There were times that she would call me and ask me to tell them that she was running late. Then she wouldn't show up at all. On the days that she would come, she'd be late, so she would ask me to unlock her door so that her students wouldn't have to wait in the hall. This also raised a problem because it meant that her students wouldn't have class. Her coworkers started complaining about her coming in so late or not showing up at all, so the head of her department would go and position himself where he could see the doors so that he would know exactly what time she got there. After she realized what he was doing, she stopped coming, period. The chair of her department called Cindy and asked her to come in and talk to him and the dean. Cindy told him no and that she wasn't coming back. Next, he called me in to talk with me about Cindy. By this time, she had told me the same thing that she was not coming back. He was concerned and asked me to go and talk to her. He told me to tell her to come in and talk to him and the dean to see if they could work something out. Dr. Newberry told me that he was going to get one of the TAs to cover my class so that I could go and talk to her now. She was at her parents' house; and when I pulled into the yard, I could see her lying on the couch in the den. When I walked to the door, I said, "Hey, girl, open up this door!" Laughing, she came to open the door and gave me a hug.

"Bitch, whatcha you doing here?" she asked.

"Came to bring you back to work," I said.

"That damn Newberry sent you to get me." She laughed.

"Yep, sure did!" I replied. "Okay, let's be real Cindy," I said matter-of-factly. "You can't just walk off the job. All Newberry wants you to do is come in and talk to him or Dean West so that you all can work something out."

"HELL NO!" she yelled. I told her that if we didn't love and care about her, it wouldn't matter, at least sleep on it. Well, by the time I'd gotten back to work, Cindy had called Newberry, talked with him, and told him that she would be in tomorrow which would be Friday. Newberry told her to take Friday off and start fresh on Monday. When I walked in, Newberry smiled and gave me a thumb up.

Sure, to her word, she was there on time Monday morning, looking and acting like her old self. I figured that she was medicated to the hilt. Whatever, she was back at work.

There were days when I could tell that she hadn't taken her medicine, and I would ask her if she remembered to take her crazy pill. She would laugh and say that she did. Then I would tell her that she didn't have a reason for the way she was acting. She'd look at me and tell me to "kiss her ass." We'd burst out laughing. I know that our coworkers didn't know what to think at times.

Things were great in the following weeks. Cindy was alert and on top of things. Well, I spoke too soon; and by the end of March, she had stopped taking her meds and was losing grip with reality. Once again, she started coming in late or not at all. I found myself trying to cover for her; and once again, Newberry called me in and told me, "You've got to stop covering for your friend." Well, we got her to start taking her meds again, but things didn't get much better. Cindy had stopped going to the department meetings. Even though they never talked about anything dealing with school, lessons, or students, they complained because Cindy stopped coming. Word soon got back to the president, and he called Dr. West to confirm the rumors. West went to the next meeting. Cindy was a no-show, and she was not on campus. Dr. West went back the following Wednesday, and Cindy wasn't in that meeting either. He went to Cindy's class room; and thank goodness, she hadn't left yet. Dr. West walked in and spoke. He asked her how she was doing and told her that she looked well. Then Dr. West told her that she was supposed to attend the department meetings. At this point, Cindy was shutting down and acted as if he wasn't there. At first, she did not acknowledge his presence at all, but she allowed him to talk. Finally Cindy told him that she didn't have time to sit and listen to them exchange recipes and talk about who's cooking what for dinner. She also told him that she didn't want to hear about whose son is dating whose daughter or why they were upset because the coach didn't play "junior" in the big game. Then she looked at Dean West and told him that he was wasting her time with that bullshit! West was speechless, got up, and left. He reported their meeting to the president, and he was not pleased at all. He told West that he was going to set up a meeting with Cindy.

That following week, Cindy was called to the president's office, and she never told me or Joyce what happened. All we know is that she was there for a long period of time.

We never knew what happened; but out of the clear blue sky in mid-April, Cindy asked me to go to the retirement office with her. I thought that this was kind of odd because we always said that we would retire at the same time. "Sure," I told her, and then I can check on my benefits while we're there. It was Thursday, so we decided to take off the following Tuesday.

We laughed and talked the entire drive to Greensboro; and before we knew it, we were pulling up into the parking lot. We walked in, signed in, and sat down waiting to be called. We had to go in separate rooms and talk to a representative. It didn't take long before we were called back. I asked the woman how many years did I have and how much I would receive each month if I were to retire now. I found out that I could retire, receive my benefits, and still work. I didn't have to do it now; I could do it at any time and receive full benefits because I had over thirty years—um, food for thought. When we got back in the car, Cindy told me that she would have twenty-eight years at the end of the school year and that she was retiring. At first, I thought she meant that she was going to retire and go back to work. I said, "That's good. You can get two checks."

She said, "No, I am coming out for good." I was floored! I could not believe what I had just heard. Later I found out through the grapevine that Cindy was given the option of retiring or being fired.

Chapter 11

Where Is Cindy?

August was here, and it was time to get into work mode. I moved around like a robot because I really missed Cindy. Again, she went off the radar, and I didn't see or hear from her. It was hard not knowing what was going on. Was she all right? Was she off her meds? Her daughter, Samantha, who was now married and living out of state called, looking for her mother. I told her that I hadn't heard from or seen Cindy in quite a while. Now, she was worried and wanted to know if she needed to come home. I told her that Joyce and I would try to find out what was going on and get in touch with her. This eased her mind a little bit, but I could tell that she was still upset.

I called Joyce; and we went riding, going to places where Cindy was known to frequent. Nothing! No one had seen or heard from her. We were near frantic and didn't know what to think or do. We kept calling her phone, no answer. It's been over a week and a half, and no one had seen or heard from her. Not knowing what to do and at wits' end, we contacted her ex-husband Nathan. We filled him in on what was going on, and he told us to give him a day or so and that he would let us know something. Sure enough, he called me the next day and said that she was in Knoxville, Tennessee. He had a friend of his at the sheriff's office track her car. She was at a motel there. He gave me the address, and I called Joyce and told her to get up and get dressed because Nathan had found Cindy or at least her car. I picked up Joyce, and we hit the road. Knoxville was at least a three to four-hour drive. So we decided to leave around eight that morning which meant that we would get there around eleven or twelve o'clock give or take a few.

I didn't want to call Samantha until I knew for sure what the situation was. Nathan told us that she was staying at a cheap motel called the Peacock. After driving around, looking for a Peacock Motel and getting lost a couple of times, we finally found the motel. What a dump! This motel looked like something from those horror shows. We were looking for Norman Bates to show up at any time. We drove around, looking for her car. We found it parked on the side of the motel in front of room 121 which we hoped was the room she was in. I parked the car, and we got out and walked up to room 121 and knocked on the door. We could hear crying coming from inside the room. "Cindy, Cindy," I called as I knocked on the door. "It's us, Brett and Joyce. Please open the door." When she didn't respond, Joyce went to the office to get a manager to open the door. We explained to him what was going on; and after he heard her crying, he unlocked the door. Lord, the odor that hit us in the face when we opened the door was enough to make you puke. The room was filthy and smelly, just downright disgusting and so was Cindy. She was sitting on the floor in a corner of the room, crying uncontrollably in what appeared to be vomit. The room had one bed with soiled sheets, a dimly-lit lamp, a TV that looked like something my grandmother might have watched in her day, and a bathroom that I wouldn't send my worst enemy to. We got her off the floor and sat her on the edge of the bed. As I tried to calm her down, I looked in Cindy's purse and found her meds and gave her a dose. We pulled the spread up over the soiled sheets and had her to lie down at the foot of the bed. Joyce called the office and asked if someone from house-keeping could come and clean the room. Some young girl came and said that she had been trying to get in to clean the room, but the lady would never let her in. We told her that we understood and asked her to start with the bathroom. In the meantime, Joyce went around the corner to the Dollar General to get some clean clothes, a toothbrush, toothpaste, soap, towels, and washcloths. As the girl was finishing up the bathroom, Joyce walked in with the clothes and towels. We got her up and took her to the bathroom. By this time, the meds were beginning to work, and she got into the shower and started washing the crud off her. While she showered, I called Samantha and Nathan to let them know that everything was all right. I told Samantha that I would make sure that Cindy called her later. We gathered Cindy's things as the girl changed the bed, cleaned, and mopped the floor. By the time she came out of the bathroom, she was looking and acting as if nothing had happened. Joyce and I looked at each other, thinking the same thing, *Cindy was getting worst.*

When we got ready to leave, we discovered that something was wrong with Cindy's car, so we called Nathan and told him that something was wrong with Cindy's care. We couldn't get it to start. He told us that he would take care of it. We got into my SUV and started our journey home. On the way, we stopped to get something to eat. It was some mom and pop restaurant, but the food was delicious, or either we were starving. Joyce drove home, and it seemed like we were at home in no time. We didn't press the issue with Cindy about why she left. I figured that she would tell me when she got good and ready.

Chapter 12

The Kiss

As soon as we got back, Cindy contacted Robert. He came a running. Brenda was still dating Robert; and when she heard that Cindy was back, she came rushing over to check on Cindy. She filled Cindy in on what was going on with her and Robert. Same old same old, he saw her when he wanted to, which she figured wasn't quite enough.

On top of all the drama with Robert, Brenda was beginning to realize that as RJ got older, she was finding out that she needed more room for all of his things. In one of her conversations with Cindy, Brenda mentioned that she needed more space because they were outgrowing their apartment. Cindy was thinking that she might be able to kill two birds with one shot while helping Brenda to solve her problem. Since her mother's passing, she had been spending more time at her father's house, helping to take care of him. She told Brenda that she could rent her house because she was planning to move in with her daddy.

That would be perfect, she thought. Talks were done, arrangements made, contracts signed, and it was a done deal. Guess who wasn't homeless and living out of the back of his truck anymore? This was the perfect setup. Cindy's parents' house was about a half mile from her house so that made it very convenient for Robert and Cindy, especially since Cindy's father, Mr. Smalls, was someone who

Robert looked up to and admired. He was always stopping by to sit and chat with him, the perfect cover.

Well, things couldn't have been going better for Cindy and Robert; but as with any good thing, it comes to an end eventually. I guess that it was time for Cindy and Robert's to end. This day, RJ was riding with his daddy when they went by Aunt Cindy's house. RJ loved his Aunt Cindy and liked visiting her whenever he could. They stayed for a while. RJ was running, playing, and talking with Mr. Smalls. Mr. Smalls loved when young children came to visit because if he felt down, they always cheered him up, made him laugh, and this made him feel better. "Let's go, buddy," called Robert. RJ gave Mr. Smalls a hug and ran to get into the back seat of the truck to get buckled in. Before Robert got into the truck, he leaned over and kissed Cindy on the lips. *Harmless*, they thought because RJ was too young to recognize things like that. Nothing was ever said until a couple of weeks later when RJ and Brenda were watching TV. A commercial came on that showed a man and woman kissing, so RJ starts pointing, laughing, and yelling, "Daddy and Aunt Cindy were kissing like that." Brenda was shocked to say the least. She questioned RJ to make sure that he knew what he was talking about. After all, he was just four years old. He might have been just four, but he was positive about what he saw. This bugged the life out of Brenda for days.

At work, she could not concentrate, thinking about what RJ had told her. Carol could see that something was bothering her, so Carol asked Brenda what was wrong. She told her what happened; and from the look on Carol's face, Brenda knew that she was keeping something from her. "Okay, Carol, out with it," demanded Brenda.

"Well, I don't know how true it is, but I've heard nigga talk about Robert and Cindy being romantically involved," she confessed. She also went on to tell her that "people have been talking and laughing at you behind your back. I do not know how long this was supposed to have been going on. But from what I've heard, it's been a while." How could Cindy do this to her, her friend, the one she told everything to about her and Robert. She was like the older sister that she never had. To think that all this time, she was some kind of joke to them, this made her furious!

Brenda was livid, but she played her part well. You know how they say, "Never let them see you sweat." So she was cool, calm, and collective. She continued crying on Cindy's shoulder while still being the loving and devoted girlfriend to Robert. But unbeknownst to them, she was plotting her revenge against Cindy. She loved Robert too much to believe that he would treat her that way, so it had to be Cindy "making" him do these things to her. Work was out of the question for Brenda right now. So when they were at work, she slept so that she could stay up all night following them.

She had gotten to a point where she couldn't function at work because they consumed her every thought. Her job sent her to open a continuing education online school in Hillsboro which kept her busy for a while. But she couldn't concentrate and stay focus on the job. She kept forgetting key elements of what she was doing and eventually was suspended. Brenda didn't care because this gave her the time she needed to keep an eye on Cindy and Robert. When her suspension was up, she still couldn't function, which ended in her being terminated. Brenda didn't care about that either because she was free to roam the streets and keep an eye on the lovebirds. She would park on side streets by Robert's job or turn up at Cindy's house on a whim. It was becoming creepy. The girl was slowly losing her mind and, in the meantime, was causing Cindy to become jumpy and restless. At night, Brenda would ride around Cindy's father's house until late in the wee hours of the morning to make sure that Robert's car wasn't there. She had become obsessed with catching them and would not let it rest. When Cindy realized that Brenda was following and watching her, she became frustrated and afraid and told Robert her suspicions. She would not sleep and spend the night sitting in front of the picture window in the living room. Sure enough there was Brenda driving slowly, back and forth, up and down the street in front of her dad's house the majority of the night. Knowing this, Robert parked his car somewhere else and walk there or have someone drop him off.

The next day, Cindy was not good for anything. One night in particular, Brenda made a bold move and stopped at Cindy's. Cindy was in her bathroom, washing her hair when she heard the backdoor doorbell. Her father was already sleeping on the other end of the house and didn't hear the bell. Cindy grabbed a towel to wipe the shampoo from her face and eyes as she walked to answer the door. The doorbell rang again. This time, Cindy yelled, "Just a minute." It was Brenda, standing there with one hand in her jacket pocket. She let her in and told her to wait in the den while she rinsed the shampoo out of her hair. She left Brenda in the den and walked back to the bathroom in her room. When she stepped out of the bathroom, there was Brenda standing in the middle of her room with her hand still in her pocket. Brenda talked to Cindy, asking her about Robert and did she know where he was. All this time, she never took her eyes off Cindy, nor did she take her hand out of her pocket. Brenda looked around the room a couple of times before leaving with her hand still in her pocket. Cindy called me as soon as Brenda left and told me what happened. Putting two and two together, we reached the conclusion that Brenda might have had a gun in her pocket and came hoping to find her and Robert together, planning to kill them.

Later we found out through the grapevine that she did have a gun that night in her pocket. We also found out that Brenda indeed had metal issues and that she told Carol that she didn't care nothing about going to jail. She would get out; her mother would see to that. She knew that this friend would make sure that this message got back to Cindy. Hearing that and remembering how Brenda acted that night when she came to the house made Cindy stop and think about her relationship with Robert. She backed away from Robert; and this time, she said that it was for good.

Chapter 13

Frances

It took a while before Cindy got over being "terrorized" by Brenda. She stayed true to her word and stayed away from Robert. She started hanging out more with an old friend of hers, Frances Kirkland, from back in the day. Frances had been living in Florida and decided to move back home after getting in trouble for drugs which caused her to lose her job. Matter of fact, Frances is Cindy's old lover Jim's sister. Talk about a piece of work! Frances was a tall slender girl with a short afro. She was a tad bit lighter than Cindy. She was a known crackhead and would do anything for drugs, and I mean anything. She began hanging out with Cindy, hitting the clubs, drinking, and doing what they did best, flirting with the guys. Frances missed the fast pace of Miami and was looking for something exciting to get into. Well, her answer was just around the corner.

A group of "rich" prominent white men from the surrounding area had recently opened a "hunting lodge." They would go there to kickback, drink, unwind, and have a good ole time. Well, it was said that they hired black women to come dance, strip, and provide sexual pleasures for them. By now, you know where this is going. One of the women was Frances. She was the most sought-after woman in the group because like I said, she would do anything for a hit. Girl, she had one of the men wrapped around her little finger. He had to have her and would do anything for her, too bad he was a married man. As a matter of fact, Bob Lawson was married to one of my coworkers, Janie. They owned an import/export business that did trading around the world. Frances had a good thing going until she and Bob came down with the same rare infection. Talk about a scandal. Well, this was one with a capital S! Janie, Bob's wife, was talking about how sick her husband was and that he had to be placed in an isolated ward away from the other patients. One of the other ladies overheard the conversation and said that she had a friend in the isolated ward too. Janie asked her what she was in there for. She said, "I think that it has to do with some type of infection too."

"Really," Janie said. You could see the wheels in Janie's head turning. Well, I knew what was going on because Cindy had filled me in on the story. Lord, I could not wait to get to Cindy to tell her the latest gossip.

By the next day, Janie and her sister, Lois Carson, had begun investigating and were beginning to make the connection. To validate their suspicions, they went to the good "ole boys" to find out what was going on between Bob and Frances. Everything came spilling out, that they wanted to know and that they didn't. That put Janie and her sister Lois on the warpath. Janie and Lois did everything that they could think of to try and run Frances out of town. With the backing of her family, Frances stood strong and did not back down. After a long stay in the hospital, Frances and Bob were released. Frances and Bob made full recoveries, and the hunting club was in full swing with a new crop of ladies. This lasted only a short time, and the hunting club became a fading memory. St. Paul was finally back to normal by their standards.

After Frances's long stint in the hospital, she tried to stop using drugs, but she just couldn't do it by herself. Cindy suggested that she consider going to a rehab center. She told Cindy that she would consider it after some soul-searching and realizing that this would be the best thing if she wanted to get her life back on track. Everyone was so proud of her for taking the first step. Cindy and Frances's family visited her every chance they got and continued to let her know that they loved her, supported her, and how proud they were of her. Frances completed the program and became one of St. Paul's model citizens. She was doing great and had even gotten a job as a salesperson at the local bridal shop.

Then one day, out of the clear blue sky, she got a phone call from an old high school boyfriend, Ben Glover. She wondered why she would be getting a call from him when she hadn't heard from him in about three years or more. During that time, he had gotten married and had a child. "Hi, stranger," she cooed into the phone.

"Hey, beautiful," he said. "What's going on?" he asked.

"Nothing, not a thing." Finally, she said, "Cut the bullshit! What do you want?"

"I just thought about you and decided to give you a call." *Yeah sure*, Frances thought.

"Okay, Ben, what is the real reason for this call?" Frances asked.

"I don't want to get into it over the phone," he replied. "Could you meet me tomorrow at the school gym around 5:30 in the evening?"

Frances told him, "Sure, no problem. I'll see you then." Now, she knew that Ben was up to something but what? She could barely sleep that night, trying to figure out what could Ben want. She tossed and turned the rest of the night.

At work the next day, she could not concentrate because she was still thinking about that call from Ben. She knew that deep down inside that it was something that she would regret later on because Ben was trouble with a capital T! She left work a little early so that she could go by the house to freshen up before meeting Ben. She arrived there about five minutes before he did and was looking in the mirror to make sure that her hair and makeup were just right. Ben pulled up, parked, and got out of his car. He walked over to Frances's car, motioned for her to unlock the door on the passenger side, and got in. Ben gave Frances a hug and a kiss on the cheek. There was the usual small talk; but after a few minutes, Frances told Ben to cut the crap and get to the point. "I know that you didn't ask me to meet you here to discuss the weather and my weave. Get to the point!"

It seems that Ben, who was a known drug dealer, needed a "mule" to help him transport drugs across state lines from Georgia. "You must be out of your fucking mind," she yelled!

"Wait a minute. Before you make up your mind, the money is good." Ben knew that he could eventually get her to do it. That's why he called her. He would let her rant and rave for a bit, but he knew that she was going to do it. Cindy never did say what it was that he said or did to get her to go along with the plan, nor did she say how much money she made. Regardless, she went along with the plan.

Cindy told her that she didn't have to do it. She said, "I know, but it's a hell of a lot of money."

"Okay, as long as you know what you might be getting yourself into."

They left late one Friday night after Cindy got home from work. They rode for about five hours until they reached their destination, a town on the other side of Atlanta. They turned off the main highway and drove about ten miles down a dark dirt road deep into the woods. They pulled up in front of a broken-down house that looked like a shack. There was no visible light from the outside, but evidently Ben had been here before and knew exactly where to go. He knocked three times on the door, and this big brut of a man opened the door and let us in. The room was dimly lit with candles and a lantern. There were only a couple of chairs and a table in the room. There was a fireplace, but it was not being used. "This her?" he asked.

"Yeah…yeah, man, this her," Ben answered.

"Come on let's get started so we can get outta here." Later, Frances found out that he was known as Big T. Big T told her to take her clothes off and get on the table. As she started taking off her clothes, Ben and Big T were putting on latex gloves. She got on the table, and they started putting condoms filled with drugs inside of her. Then they taped the rest all over her body. She had drugs all over her. Frances said that she had drugs in places that she didn't know that she had.

"Hurry and get dressed," Big T commanded. Stiff and barely able to move, she did as she was told. Next, Ben and T whispered something to each other; Ben grabbed Frances by the arm and helped her to the car. It was an uncomfortable ride home, but finally she just drifted off to sleep. When she woke up, she didn't recognize where she was.

She asked Ben where they were, and he said, "At my house." He told her to wait in the car, and he went inside. In about five minutes, Ben came back and told her to get out and come inside. When she walked inside, she was surprised to see his wife and father-in-law standing there. His wife, Sandra, led her into a bedroom and told her to take her clothes off and lie down on the bed. She put on latex gloves and proceeded to remove the bags of drugs from inside of her. "Lord, please don't let them burst. Lord, please don't let them burst!" she prayed repeatedly until all the condoms were out. They took the others from her body, and she gave a sigh of relief. She was good and ready to go home. She used the bathroom and ate some breakfast. Then Ben took her home. There was not much conversation on the way home. She did want to know what part did his wife and father-in-law have in all of this. It seems that his father-in-law, Mr. Murdaugh, was a known "kingpin" who had served time for selling drugs. When he got out of prison, he opened a deli and went legit for a while. But his old contacts kept calling him and wanting him to help them out. At the time, he didn't know that his son-in-law was a small-town drug dealer from St. Paul. After putting their heads together, they decided that they could work together and make a fortune. Ben's wife used to be one of the mules; but since she had just given birth and was nursing and the others just didn't want to do it anymore, they had to find someone else. Ben never wanted his wife to do it; and since they had started a family, that was out of the question. That's were Frances came in. Ben knew that he would be able to get her to do.

Frances, against her better judgment, made a couple more runs with Ben and made up her mind that this one that they were making on Saturday was going to be her last run. Same old same old, but this time was going to turn out differently. They made it to North Carolina safe and sound. They met with Mr. Murdaugh's contact, followed the same routine and left. On the way back to North Carolina, Frances told Ben that this was her last run with him. She was through before something bad happens, and she ends up in jail. Well, no sooner than she spoke, those words they were pulled over. The sweat started pouring off them as if they were standing in a rainstorm. Someone must have tipped them off because they had the K9 unit with them. When they saw them, they knew that they were up shit creek without a paddle. Since they were carrying so much, it didn't take long for the K9 to sniff it out. They knew that no explanation could help them, so off to jail they went. Ben called his wife, and Frances called her mother, Mrs. K. Well, they were arraigned the next day, and bond was set at $100,000. Sandra was there to post Ben's bond, and he was released until his trial date. No one ever showed up for Frances, so she had to sit in jail. Frances never did get out on bond because her family didn't show up until she had been in jail for about four months. Mrs. K along with Cindy went to visit her. She looked a mess. She had lost weight, and her weave was beginning to look matted. When she saw them, she broke down and cried. She told them that her hearing was in three weeks and that she hoped that they would be there to support her. Well, either they forgot or just didn't care, but no one was there. The judge sentenced her to one year and suspended it to six months and two years proba-tion upon her release, and she had to complete one hundred hours of community service. Time went by fast; and before she knew it, she was walking through the prison gates and into freedom, something she would never take for granted again.

When she told Cindy all that she endured, she couldn't help but laugh. "It was tough," she said, but she laughed and said, "What doesn't kill you makes you stronger." Cindy brought her up to date on what was going on with her and her situation with Robert, which was nothing at the time being.

Well, swearing off men, Cindy, Frances, Shelia, and Linda Stone, an old classmate of Frances, decided to do their own thing because men had left a bad taste in their mouth, and they could do better without them. You would see the four of them together all the time that summer. By this time, Cindy's father had died, and she was left alone in the house. Her father's death didn't affect her as much as her mother's did. She was able to function and get on with life.

Chapter 14

Sex Tapes

Before the sex tapes surfaced, rumors were already circulating about so-called orgies that the four of them were having. The four of them would have these private parties, and only the who's who of the ghetto fab crowd was invited. Cindy's house became *the* party house. At any given day or night, something was going on there. They were drinking and getting high all the time. Nothing mattered to them except having a good time.

This is supposedly when these sex tapes started surfacing of them having orgies. Then somehow, the men got wind of it and wanted to join in. At first, they would just happen to be in the neighborhood and decided to drop by. Before long, they were joining in on the fun. Joyce and I believe that that was how the tapes came to surface. The men were filming them and made copies to sell. They supposedly had girl-on-girl sex, three-and-four-way girl sex, and one man or men and the four of them. They say it was unbelievable at some of the things that they did. They even took the time to give the tapes names. "The Black Hole" and "Playing with Kitty" were a couple of the titles that were told to me and Joyce. It took me and Joyce the longest to get a copy; and after we got one, we were sorry that we did. It made us physically sick, and we never did watch all of it. They were underground, and that's where they needed to stay. Anyway, we didn't judge Cindy because we knew deep down inside that Cindy was crying for help, and she was probably off her meds again. We never asked her about it. She would have lied and denied it just the same.

During one of their "parties" which consisted of male and female now, Cindy met Paul, and they somehow made a connection. He was a tall slender man that you could tell worked out. He was very friendly and pleasing to look at. Paul was a friend of Shelia whom she met when he would come down to visit his aunt. He was a frequent visitor at Cindy's parties, and this brought them closer and closer; and before long, they were an item.

Joyce and I didn't really know Paul. He moved to New York at an early age and lived there most of his life. He just recently moved back to St. Paul. We heard about him through mutual friends and family members. All we knew was that Paul seemed to make Cindy happy, and that was enough for us. They both liked to travel; and since she was retired and he was out of work and collecting unemployment, they stayed in the road. Since he wasn't working, everybody, including me and Joyce, felt that he was living off of her. In casual conversation, I brought the subject up once with her and she told me that I didn't have anything to do with it and to mind my damn business, which I did and never brought it up again. It wasn't soon before she had moved Paul in to live with her. Once they were staying together, the "parties" were a thing of the past. Things seemed to be going good for the two of them until we heard talk that Paul had a wife, Joan, and son living on the other side of town. Here I go again sticking my nose where it didn't belong, and I asked Cindy had she heard anything about Paul having a wife and child. Cindy knew the woman and her son and didn't have a problem with them. Well, before Paul moved in with Cindy, he was living with his sister and creeping with Joan who we found out was never married to Paul and had him paying child support for a child that was not his. He confessed to Cindy that he knew that Chad wasn't his son, but the boy had been calling him daddy all his life. He didn't have the heart to make a stink about it. She understood and didn't pursue it anymore.

Chapter 15

Doug

As soon as things seemed to be going good for Cindy, Joyce was going through her personal hell with Doug. Doug was from Joyce's hometown of Greenville, North Carolina. They knew each other from school and from around town. After graduating from high school, each went in different directions and lost touch with each other. Joyce was dating her high school sweetheart and drinking buddy, Harry Black, and they eventually got married. They drank and partied hearty. It got to a point that Harry was jealous of her flirting and started hitting her. He didn't want her out there partying with him anymore. She stayed home and began to drink even more. When Harry was at work, Joyce would get together with the girls and drink, smoke, and get high. A year later after their marriage, Joyce was pregnant. This caused her to slow down with the partying, and she stopped drinking cold turkey. Harry stopped hitting her. In November, Joyce gave birth to healthy twin girls. She and Harry were ecstatic! He still drank, but he was trying to cut back. For a while, everything was going great. Harry was the loving husband and was very attentive to Joyce; and then one day, he saw her talking to Doug who had just recently moved back to town. Harry couldn't stand to see that so he went drinking and came home sloppy drunk. He must have forgotten that Joyce had recently given birth and began beating her, just so happened her brother, Mike Owens, was coming to check on her and heard his sister inside crying and pleading for her life.

The babies were crying in the background. Mike kicked in the door just in time and grabbed Harry and knocked him out. If he hadn't, who knows what would have happened to Joyce and the babies. Mike called the cops and had Harry arrested. One of the policeman rushed Joyce to the hospital, and they admitted her. The babies were all right. So Mike called his mother, Mrs. Owens, to come and get them. He was going to stay with Joyce. They wanted to keep her for a couple of days to make sure that she was going to be all right.

When the doctor felt that she was out of the woods, she was released. Mike picked her up and took her to their parents' house where she stayed with the babies. Harry would call, pleading and begging for her to forgive him and come home. He promised that he would stop drinking and would never lay another hand on her.

Taking baby steps, she would let him come and visit the babies at her parents' house. Mike was always there to make sure that he didn't touch her. Joyce began to see a change in Harry, and he adored the babies. Soon Joyce was taking the babies to their trailer to visit Harry. She began spending nights over there; and before long, she and the babies had moved back in. Everything was going good, and Joyce seemed happy. Then Harry got laid off from his job. Sitting around all day with nothing to do but listen to the babies crying and Joyce complaining, Harry found silence at the bottom of a bottle. First, it was a beer here and there, then a glass or two of whiskey. Finally he was drinking a bottle of whiskey a day and sometimes even more. Joyce saw the signs of what was going to happen next, but she tried to put it out of her mind. One Friday night, he went out with some of the fellas from where he used to work. They had heard that the boss was going to call everybody back to work, and they were having an early celebration. The call never came, so he began to take his frustrations out on Joyce. It's a good thing that the girls were too young to understand what was going on. This went on until Joyce had enough and called Mike to help her move back home to her parents. Mike came and took them to the house. Then he went back to the trailer with a couple of his friends, and they gave Harry the beating of his life. This time, there was no going back for Joyce. About two weeks later, the trailer caught on fire with Harry inside, and he was burned to death. They seemed to think that Harry had been drinking and went to sleep or passed out with a lit cigarette in his hand and dropped it on the carpet in the bedroom. Nigga talk says that Joyce and Mike set the fire and made it look like an accident. Nonetheless, the trailer went up in flames, and he didn't get out. About six months after the funeral, Joyce and the girls moved to St. Paul where she bought a government house for her and the girls, Harriet and Henrietta. Since she wasn't working and she had applied for Harry's benefits, she got the house for little or nothing per month. She had enough money left from the insurance policy to pay bills until the social security checks started the following month.

Chapter 16

Kevin

Joyce started drinking heavily and going to clubs and parties. The girls were staying with Harry's mother because of Joyce's lifestyle. If she was sober enough on any given day, she would go and visit the girls. They would be happy to see her but enjoyed staying with the grandmother. Joyce would bring them home, but they would cry and beg to go back to the grandmother's house. They were only about three, so this gave Joyce free time to do her thing. By this time, she was seeing Kevin regularly. He knew about the twins and would ask about them constantly. He told her that they should be with her. She took what he said to heart and started trying to clean up her act and bring her girls home. She continued seeing Kevin, and he began spending nights there. The girls loved him, and Joyce thought that she had found her "man."

Before long, the girls were going to school, and this gave Joyce nothing but free time. She heard that the community college needed bus drivers for their outreach program and was giving bus-driving training classes. She said, "What the hey." And signed up for the classes. She passed the classes and got her CDL license. In January, they gave her a bus route. She enjoyed having something to do, and it also allowed her to interact with the students and faculty at the school. This is how Cindy and I met Joyce. Well, Cindy knew of her and had some dealings with her in passing. She latched on to us because we were the youngest black teachers out there. We didn't mind. Joyce was a lot of fun. She even started taking a few classes during her free time.

The years passed; and before we knew it, Harriet and Henrietta were sixteen. She said that she had to get a job, so she applied for an assistant job at the college. They hired her at the beginning of the next school term as a computer lab TA. She loved it because it made her feel as if she was a teacher. The students did not like her at all. They said that she was too mean. Other than that, things were going great. She felt that everything in her life was on track. The girls, she, and Kevin were doing good. There is always a calm before the storm, and hers was about to hit.

Kevin had lost his job for going to work drunk and was sitting around all day, doing nothing. He would spend most of his time hanging out at the corner pantry/pool hall. There he met Tricia. Tricia was twenty-two, cute as a button, and sweet as could be. I knew her because I worked with her at a camp one summer. Her mother worked at the day care around the corner. Tricia and Kevin would talk when she was on duty and formed a friendship that eventually led to them dating. When he became serious with Tricia, he broke it off with Joyce. Joyce lost her everlasting mind.

Joyce was on the warpath. She was going to get Kevin back by any means necessary. She talked to the girl's mother at the day care; she would call her at home, telling her about Kevin. Kevin was no good. He's just using Tricia, and you need to tell her to stop seeing him. She bashed him from one end of town to the other to anybody that knew him and would listen. Since this wasn't working, she decided to take matters into her own hands. Joyce must not have been thinking about the end results before going to Tricia's job and calling her out. Tricia at first tried to ignore her, and then she asked her to leave before she called the cops. Joyce wasn't hearing any of this and continued to belittle and cuss Tricia. Tricia called her mother, and that just added fuel to the fire for Joyce. She grabbed Tricia and started hitting her. Not to be outdone, Tricia started hitting as good as she was getting. One of the customers in the store called the cops because no one seemed able to break them up. By the time the cops got there, Joyce with her old behind was rolling around on the floor, fighting this twenty-two-year-old girl. The cops were in the process of breaking up the fight by the time Tricia's mother arrived. It was a time. Tricia didn't press charges against Joyce, but she was banned from going to that store. This didn't win Kevin back; and after that, Tricia stopped seeing him too.

The news of Joyce rolling around on the floor fighting a girl young enough to be her daughter didn't sit too well with the college where she worked. They couldn't just fire her because no charges were made, but they did warn her and place her on probation. The next thing we knew they were doing away with the TA in the computer lab. Joyce was out of a job, but she still drove bus for the school. It was never the same because a lot of the school's people began to shun her. So there she was again, alone without a man in her life, but she was determined that she was not going to let this setback force her to start drinking again. She enjoyed working in the lab at the community college, so she decided to apply at other colleges in the area.

No one had any openings at the time; and if one did, they had a waiting list. She decided to try other fields of work. She finally landed a job as a dispatcher, a 911 operator. This was her calling. She could keep up with the latest news. Plus she was helping people. She is still employed there.

Chapter 17

The Fourth of July

Before we knew it, it was the fourth of July weekend. Joyce had the weekend off, and one of her coworkers was having this big fourth of July celebration and invited all of them to come. Evelyn and her family were famous for their fourth of July celebrations, and not many folks turned down an invite to one of them. Joyce and the girls were excited about going.

Since the fourth was on a Sunday, they were having it that Saturday the third. It usually starts around 2:00 in the afternoon with fireworks after dark. Cindy, Paul, Chris, and I got there around two as they were placing the first group of food on the tables. They had everything you could think of, fried fish, hot dogs, ribs, bar-be-que pork, hamburgers, shrimp, oysters, lobster, crabs, salads of all kinds, fruits. You name it. It was there, and everything was always nice and hot. There were beverages of all kinds, soda, juices, water, wines, beers of all brands, and liquors.

By the time Joyce and the girls got there a little after three, Cindy and I were going back for seconds and thirds. We told her to get there early. Next time she'll know what early is. Henrietta and Harriet saw some of their friends and went to join them. Joyce came to where we were in line. Joyce was so amazed at all the food that she didn't know where to start, not a problem for me and Cindy. We told her, "It is food. Just start in the middle and work your way out." We laughed.

By the time the fireworks started, we were stuffed like pigs. We couldn't do a thing, just sit and enjoy the show. Joyce went to get some water and literally bumped into Donald, a cousin of Evelyn. He introduced himself to Joyce and asked her if she was new in town because he didn't remember seeing her at any of the other celebrations. She told him that she wasn't new in town since she and the girls had lived in St. Paul for over ten years. She also told him that this was the first fourth of July celebration that she had attended. By the time she got back to us, she had found her dream man.

Donald had an associate degree in welding from one of the technical colleges. He was good at what he did and made a decent living at it. He headed one of the departments at Steele's Welding where he worked. Donald was an attractive man. He stood six feet, nice built with a full beard, and he kept his head bald which made him look even more distinguished.

The man had a walk on him that made the women's hearts skip a beat every time he passed. Even though Donald was a good person, he was also a player and master manipulator of woman. He had been married and divorced because of his wandering eye and a brief affair that he had. Luckily they didn't have any children while they were married.

In the weeks to come, Donald and Joyce talked constantly on the phone. They were trying to get together for a date; but with their difficult schedules, it was almost impossible. Then out of the clear blue sky as if by fate, they had a weekend free at the same time. The state fair was in town so they had their first date there. They had a ball; and from that moment on, Donald was the topic of conversation. We even had to hear about their sex life. Lord, the first time she described her first encounter of oral sex with Donald almost made me throw up. No one wants to hear that, especially when you are trying to eat. Donald and his brother were renting an apartment together, but they had a rule. So Joyce said Donald told her about not having woman sleeping over since it was one house down from their parents' house. After a while, Joyce let him move in with her and the girls. Cindy and I didn't feel that she should have done that and told her so. Her girls were teenagers now, and he was not their father. That was a short-lived conversation, and Donald was the new man of the house. The two of them did everything together, and Joyce worshipped the ground he walked on. During this time, we believe that she forgot that she had children. She would make plans for her and Donald, leaving the children home to fend for themselves. They would call me and Cindy, wanting to know if we knew where their mother was. It was beginning to turn into a sad situation.

He changed everything about Joyce; I must admit that some were for the better. Donald told her how to dress and what to cook. He also talked her into going into debt to buy a new car. She did need one, but she could have made it another year with her car until she was well on her feet. She got the car thinking that he was going to help her with the payment or at least with the household bills. He told her that it wasn't his house or his car, and he was not paying any bills for anything. But he drove the car more than she did. She thought that that was something big. Her man was driving her car. He would drop her off at work and keep the car. Most times, she would end up hitchhiking home. We told her that she was being ridiculous and that she needed to wise up. Joyce was not hearing that because she was in love, and he was good for her.

Things began to get a little tough around the house because they cut Joyce's hours at work. Donald still wasn't helping with the bills. He would buy food occasionally because he didn't really care for Joyce's cooking or the quality of foods that she bought. So he would go out and buy what he liked to eat and cook it himself. He wasn't selfish in that aspect, and they were welcome to join him. The girls liked his cooking better than their mother's.

Pushed into a corner because her bills were getting behind, she went to a loan company and took out a huge loan to pay off the car and, believe it or not, Donald's truck. Now we knew that she had lost her everlasting mind or to put it into Cindy's words, "her fucking mind!" Cindy figured that she needed one of her "crazy pills." This was one time that I had to agree. Then she decided that she and Donald were going on a cruise. No, she wasn't taking the girls. She made arrangements with her brother to come and stay with them while they were gone. The girls called me and asked if they could stay with me. "Sure, as long as it's all right with your mother." I knew that it wouldn't be a problem with Joyce, but I still wanted them to check with her first. Joyce said that it was fine, so the girls spent the week with me. The girls had a great time, and I let them invite some of their friends over to spend the weekend with them.

This was the first time Joyce and Donald had been on a cruise; and according to Joyce, they had so much fun. Donald just sat back and enjoyed. After all, Joyce was paying for everything. At least she remembered to get the girls souvenirs.

The next month, she was rolling coins, trying to pay her light bill. We told her to tell Donald that she needed help with paying the utility bill. She didn't say how much the bill was, but he gave her twenty-five dollars. Shoot! He should have paid the whole thing. You would have thought he did from the way she went on which I didn't see was anything to brag on; but if she was satisfied, then I was overjoyed.

When things started going bad between him and Joyce, Donald moved back with his brother. Joyce didn't know it, but he was still paying his part of the rent there. That rule he told Joyce that he and his brother had about bringing women there was a lie because he would meet his ladies there from time to time. Finally he just started staying there, period. He would spend a night here and there with Joyce, but he was not going to take on Joyce's problems or her bills. He left a few of his things over there to give Joyce the illusion that he was still living there. He sure didn't have a problem bringing his laundry there for her to do; and like a fool, she would do it.

We told Joyce to open her eyes. "Donald is just using you." He's seeing someone else, and we bet she's not doing all this stuff for him like you are. She did not want to hear that. She figured that they needed a vacation away from St. Paul. So there she was rolling coins, trying to plan another cruise. This one fell through because he didn't want to go on another one. Something was wrong, but she just couldn't figure out what it was. Henrietta and Harriet, even though they liked Donald, was glad that he wasn't coming around a lot. This began to take its toll on Joyce. She would call him crying, asking if he was coming over. It got to a point that the girls called me and Cindy because they were worried about their mother crying all the time. They thought that she might have been sick or something. We tried to assure the girls that she wasn't sick and that everything was going to be okay. We tried talking with Joyce, telling her that the girls were upset because they hear her crying all the time, and they think that she is sick because she won't tell them what's wrong.

On the rare occasion that Donald would stop by and didn't stay, she would be crying and begging, trying to get him to stay. It didn't matter. She was still doing his laundry. Not wanting to deal with anymore of Joyce's drama, he just stopped going over. That didn't stop her from calling and going by his job. He tried to be polite, but it was getting more trying by the minute.

He tried to make a clean break and wouldn't take anymore of her calls. Since she wasn't allowed at his apartment, she would park on the side of the road and wait for him. It finally sunk in that things were over with them when she heard that he was engaged to a young lady that he had been seeing. This broke her heart. Now she wanted to get even. She went to his apartment early one morning when she knew he was there and demanded everything that she had bought him, suits, shoes, sweaters, pants, shirts, just whatever she had bought she took with her. Donald didn't fight her on it and let her take them because he didn't want to make a scene. He was already embarrassed, especially since Joyce was loud and the neighbors were listening and looking. To add insult to injury, Joyce went to the car wash laughing and told the guys there what she did and showed them all the clothes in her car. They had a big laugh at her and Donald. They never let him live it down. If that wasn't enough, Joyce decided that she was going to have a yard sale. So she asked a friend of hers if she could set up a table on the side of his shop and have a yard sale. He let her, and she had all of Donald's things out there, selling them. Word soon spread; and before long, there was a crowd gathering, to be nosy if not for anything else. Joyce didn't know that they had spread the word not to buy anything from her, but the fellas still had a good laugh at Donald's expense. Joyce stayed out there all day and only sold a sweater, and that was to the guy who let her set up on the side of his shop. She made herself look stupid and succeeded in pushing

Donald all the way out of her life. Boy, did they talk about her. In the town's people's eyes, she was an outsider whereas Donald was a home boy, born and bred from an outstanding, prominent family. He was always going to come out, smelling like a rose. She cried for days after that and even called Donald, trying to apologize. It fell on deaf ears. Every time she saw Donald, she cried. The girls were beginning to get tired of all the crying again.

As time went on, Donald began to be cordial to her again. Soon he was stopping by her house to check on her and the girls. Does someone smell a rat?! Long story short, he was sick, and the woman that he was engaged to left him. She told her friends that she was too young to be tied down with an old sick man.

Back to good old reliable Joyce, Donald didn't tell her that he was sick. He just played the "I missed you and realized that I wanted you, not her" card. He really laid on the bullshit! Then came the day when he wasn't feeling well and had to go to the doctor. Well, we know who went with him. He had some kind of ailment that caused them to put him in the hospital for a couple of days for treatment, and he would need bed rest for another week. Nurse Joyce at your service. She moved him back into her home and took care of him. She was as happy as a lark. As soon as he was up and about, he moved back to his place. But that didn't stop Joyce from caring for him. Oh yeah, did I forget to mention that she could go to the apartment now. Girl, she was in high cotton now!

Donald's brother had built him a house and had moved out. Donald didn't want commitment, so the apartment was fine for him. Since Joyce was his nurse maid, he would encourage her to take the night there. The bed was not comfortable for her to sleep on, and Donald had back problems. So she bought him a bed. Everything was as it should be in Joyce's eyes. Donald needed her, and she would always be there for him.

With strength came not needing Joyce as much anymore. Sure, he was still nice to her because she was doing his laundry, picking up his medicine, driving him to his appointments, and making sure that he didn't take his medicine on an empty stomach. Cindy and I told Joyce to be careful and not get caught up in Donald's web again.

She would brush us off and say, "I got this." Donald played it cool in the weeks to come, keeping in touch on a regular basis at first. Then in the weeks to follow, he would text her nothing extravagant, just a hello or "what's going on?" She would be tickled pink, but Cindy said that he was playing a game. He was texting her to make sure that she was still there for him. Little did she know that he was disrespecting her in the worst kind of way. He just wanted to make sure she was there just in case he needed her to help him out with something. He knew that he had her waiting in the wings. It didn't matter. She was hearing from her Boo Thang. She was beginning to hear rumors floating around about him seeing another woman. At first, she didn't believe it until Cindy and I purposely made sure that she saw him with the woman. We didn't know what Joyce's reaction would be, but we were tired of Donald making an ass of our friend. Through mutual friends of the woman, we found out that they were going to the movies that Friday night.

We told Joyce that we were going to do a "girls' night" Friday night. We were going to the movies and out to dinner. Cindy picked up Joyce, and they drove to my house to pick me up. We arrived early and got a good parking spot right in front of the movie theater so that we could see everything and everybody who was coming and going. We were just sitting there, laughing and talking when Donald and his girlfriend appeared, arms around each other laughing, talking, and kissing as they walked to get in line to purchase their tickets. Cindy trying to be funny said, "Brett, look at Donald and Joyce going to the movies. Oh wait, Joyce, that ain't you," and starts laughing. "YOU BITCHES SET ME UP. Y'ALL THINK THAT YOU ARE SO DAMN SMART!" she screamed. She was trying to get out the car to approach him; but Cindy, thinking ahead, cranked up the car as soon as she saw them and pulled off just in time. It was no need in trying to tell you and like they say, "One picture is worth a thousand words." We spent about an hour or so riding around, trying to calm Joyce down. After she had a good cry, that was the end of that.

Chapter 18

Paul

Cindy and Paul were doing great until we found out that he was using drugs again, and talk was that Cindy was on them too. We don't think she was using because most the time, when he got high, he would be with his friends at the drug house. He was going down fast, and Cindy was getting worried about him. In the beginning, she was helping to support his habit by giving him money. When she saw that he was getting worse, she got scared and stopped giving him money to buy the drugs with. Cindy began missing things from around the house and knew what was going on. She knew that there was no need in confronting him because she knew that he would lie. Cindy just made sure that things that were of value to her were in a safe place. Desperate one night and needing a fix, Paul did the unthinkable. He took Cindy's car and traded it to the drug dealer for crack. Chad, one of Cindy's drug-dealer friends, heard about what was going down. He called Cindy immediately. She was furious! She knew Lamont who was the local kingpin because he was a student at the school where she used to be the principal. She thought for sure that she could talk to him and explain the circumstances. "I'm sorry, Teach. No deal. This is business." Lamont continued, "Paul owes me about twenty-five hundred dollars for drugs. And when I get it, the car is yours."

"Damn, Lamont!" she yelled.

"Sorry, Teach, but you need to talk to Paul." At the time, Paul was MIA. No one knew where he was hiding.

When the talk with Lamont failed, Cindy hatched a plan with Sheila, Frances, and Linda. They were going to steal her car back from Lamont. When she told me and Joyce what she was planning to do, Lord, forgive us, but Joyce and I were glad that she didn't involve us. We asked Cindy had she thought this through, and she said that she had and that it was no need in trying to talk her out of it. She was going to get her car no matter what!

It was Wednesday, so they were going to wait until Friday night. The place would be crowded, and everybody would be so high that they wouldn't be thinking about them. Friday, around midnight, they drove up near the house where the car was parked. Cindy got out of Frances's car and sneaked up to her car. She carefully opened the door and eased inside, cranked it up, and backed out of the yard, making sure that the lights were off. The music was blasting, and the yard was full of cars. It's a good thing no one was parked behind her car. It wasn't until the next day after all the cars had cleared out before they realized that Cindy's car was gone. Thank goodness, she made it out safe and sound. When Lamont realized what had happened, he pitched a fit, but he knew that he couldn't do anything about it. So he left it alone and didn't pursue it. He couldn't report it missing or stolen because everybody knew that it was Cindy's car. He cut his lost and forgot about it.

Things were kind of normal for a while for Cindy. Paul was still missing, and we didn't know where he was. Cindy said that she didn't care; but deep down inside, we knew that she was worried. Two months after he vanished from sight, in early September, Cindy got a collect call from Paul at Charter Rivers. She hesitated because this was unexpected, but she accepted the call. She said, "Hello."

"Cindy, this is Paul. Please don't hang up," he pleaded. He started to cry. "Cindy I am so sorry for all the pain and hurt that I caused you. I just couldn't help it, I was strung out on drugs. I was in bad shape. I don't know where I ran that night, but I knew that I had to get out of town. I passed out in the yard of a family that recognized me and knew my father. When I came to, I was in the hospital. They told me that I almost died. It was hard, and I still have a long way to go. I'd never been that sick before in my life. I thought that my insides were being ripped out through my nose. The father of the family that found me was a minister, and he visited me every day I was in the hospital.

Reverend Jamison would come and pray for me and just let me talk. I told him that I needed help and that I never wanted to feel like that again. He told me that if I was serious about getting clean, he would help me get into rehab. I owe Reverend Jamison my life. It's time for me to go, but I will call you again later this week if it's all right with you."

"I'd like that," Cindy said.

They kept in constant contact, and she even went to the rehab center to see him. While there, she met Reverend Jamison. He was a kind, fatherly man. You got the impression that you could talk with him about anything. He gave Cindy his number and told her to call him anytime if she felt like talking or if she just needed prayer. Cindy called him on numerous occasions and made a point of visiting him whenever she went to see Paul.

Paul talked with Cindy about his release and what he was going to do when he got out. At the time, he wasn't sure about anything but one thing he was positive of; he was not going back to St. Paul. He told Cindy that Reverend Jamison offered to help him get a job and an apartment if he wanted to stay in Charlotte. He felt that if he went back to St. Paul, he would fall back into old habits. She understood and supported his decision one hundred percent. Then came the question: would Cindy consider moving to Charlotte with him?

Cindy called me after talking with Paul and asked me what I thought about her moving to live in Charlotte with Paul. We talked about it extensively, weighing the pros and cons. By the end of our conversation and from her tone, I could tell that she had already made up her mind and was going to move to Charlotte. I asked her had she talked with Samantha about her decision. I knew that this wasn't going to sit too good with her because she couldn't stand Paul. She informed me that she was a grown woman, and Sam didn't have anything to do with it. This was her life, and she was to live it like she wanted. "Was just asking," I said. So I left that alone and changed the subject. I just couldn't leave well enough alone and asked her if she was happy and would be satisfied leaving St. Paul. She said that she would, and it was time that she made a new start somewhere else. Charlotte really wasn't that far away from St. Paul. It was about a forty-five-minute drive, which made it about an hour from where I lived in Logan.

The week before Cindy left, Joyce and I helped her pack up her things and close the house. The night before she left, she came to Logan and stayed with me and Chris. We had a nice time; and I, not being able to take a hint, asked her again if she was sure about the move and especially about Paul. "Brett, you worry about me too much, I am sure. I'll take care of myself. I'll be all right," she assured me.

The next morning, Cindy was up bright and early and rearing to go. We sat down and had breakfast all the while talking. After breakfast, she left, and I told her to call me the minute she got to Paul's. In about an hour and a half, Cindy called to let me know that she had arrived safe and sound. Hearing the excitement in her voice, I prayed that everything was going to work out for her. She said the apartment was in a nice neighborhood and seemed to be in a nice part of town. It was kind of small, but it would serve the purpose for now.

In the weeks to follow, Cindy had gotten a job at one of the schools in the area. She was a part-time aide. She loved it because she didn't have the responsibility of a teacher. She worked in the office to help the secretary with attendance, tardiness, and the lunch count in the mornings. She was usually through by eleven unless they asked her to do something extra. This was the perfect job. It gave her something to do. Also it freed up her afternoons, and she didn't have to miss her soap operas.

Paul was on the right track too. Reverend Jamison had helped him to get a job at a corner pantry/gas station. He enjoyed the interaction with the people. And it gave him a sense of self-worth. Things were going great for the two of them. He had more hours than he could handle; and after six months, he was promoted to assistant manager. He couldn't wait to tell Cindy and Reverend Jamison. When he told Reverend Jamison, he said, "Paul, my boy, I saw great potential in you. All you needed was a hand." Paul took Cindy out on the town to celebrate. She called after their evening and told me that she had a blast!

A few months after the move, Joyce and I went to visit Cindy just to check on her and make sure that she was all right. We arrived around twelve one Saturday. Paul was at work, so it was just the three of us, and it was like old times. We ate, drank wine, talked, and laughed until we cried. We had a wonderful visit, but something wasn't right. Around four o'clock, we felt that we should be getting back on the road. Group hug, then Joyce and I were on our way.

On the way home, Joyce and I talked about our visit with Cindy. Neither one of us wanted to be the first to say anything. Even though we had a nice visit, something was off with Cindy. We just couldn't put our finger on it, but we both noticed it. I wondered if she was off her meds again. It didn't seem like that was the problem. It was something else. I told Joyce that I was going to call her when I got home. On the way, I called Sam to let her know that we were leaving Charlotte from visiting her mother. I told her everything was all right.

She told me that she was going to visit her next month in April. She had a surprise that she wanted to share with her. We guessed that she might be pregnant. Sam just laughed and said, "Stop being nosy, Aunt Brett and tell Miss Joyce the same thing." But she never confirmed or denied it. This would send Cindy over the moon with joy! This might be the news that she needed to put her back on track.

Joyce and I would make it a point of calling Cindy every day, trying to see if we could get a handle on what was going on. She would swear up and down that everything was okay. We took her at her word and left it alone.

Chapter 19

Liar!

The following month, I got a call from Paul. Cindy had collapsed, and he didn't know what was wrong. He had called 911, and the ambulance was on the way. I called Joyce, and she was on her way to Logan to pick me up so that we could go to Charlotte. I didn't call Sam because I didn't want to worry her, but I did call Nathan to let him know what had happened. I told him that I hadn't called Sam because I wanted to be able to tell her what was wrong. Joyce did some driving that afternoon; and before I knew it, we were at the hospital.

Joyce and I found Paul pacing back and forth in the hall. "What happened?" Joyce and I demanded. He was talking in circles, not making any sense at all. Then he looked at me and Joyce and said that it was all his fault.

"What did you do to her? She better not be hurt!"

"No, I didn't put a hand on her. We were arguing about this girl, Nancy, from work. I swear that there is nothing going on. We are just friends."

"So, what's the problem?" I questioned.

"Cindy overheard me talking to her and got the wrong idea."

"What idea was that?" I asked.

"I was trying to explain to Cindy when she just fell to the floor."

"That better be all there is to this story," said Joyce through clenched teeth.

"Have you seen or talked to the doctor since she arrived?"

"No! And the nurses won't tell me anything."

We went over to the nurses' station and asked, "Can you tell us what's going on with our sister, Cindy Porter?" Just as she pulled her chart and was getting ready to answer us, the doctor walked out. The nurse told her that we were Cindy's family. He said that it seems that Cindy has a heart murmur, and that along with her panic attack caused her to lose consciousness. This was her body's way of letting her know that she must start taking better care of herself. Do either of you know if she takes any other drugs in addition to her medication? "None that I know of. Paul, is she taking or doing some other drug?" Paul dropped his head and said no.

"Good, but she also needs to stop smoking. This will make her feel better and add years to her life. I want to keep her for a couple of days and monitor her heart to make sure that there is not something else going on."

"Can we see her?" I asked.

"I just gave her something to make her sleep, but you can see her for a few minutes."

We walked in fussing. "Girl, don't you scare us like that again," Joyce and I said. "Thank goodness that you are going to be all right." She looked at us and gave us a faint smile then she was out. The medicine was beginning to take effect. We sent Paul home and spent the night at the hospital.

When Joyce and I were sure that Cindy was sleeping, we said to each other that we knew something was wrong. I asked, "Do you think Paul is telling the truth?"

"Hell no! That nigga is lying through those damn yellow teeth, well, at least the ones he has left." We forgot where we were and fell out laughing. We made up our minds that we were going to investigate his so-called story before we left. Also we thought that he answered kind of slow when the doctor asked about her being on any other drugs. Something's just not right.

Paul was there bright and early the next morning. He wanted to check on Cindy before he went to work. He asked us if he could talk to Cindy alone for a minute. We told him that we were going downstairs to get breakfast. I wondered what he has to say so that we couldn't hear it. "He better be apologizing out of that yuck mouth." We laughed. He came down to the cafeteria, gave us a hug, and told us not to worry because he was going to take care of Cindy. We told him that he better, or else he had us to answer to. We told him to call us later and tell us how she was doing.

After eating, we went back to Cindy's room to talk with her before leaving. When we walked in, she was sitting up, eating her breakfast and greeted us with "hello, bitches!" We hugged her and almost cried because she was looking better than she did yesterday. And she was sounding like the old Cindy.

After talking and catching up with the latest gossip, we got to the business at hand. "What's going on with you and Paul?"

She got this funny look on her face and asked, "What do you mean?"

"Cindy, this is us you're talking to. We want the truth."

She took a deep breath and started talking slow at first, sounding like someone else. Then in her regular tone, she said, "Paul is seeing some bitch at work. He says that they are just friends, but I know better."

We didn't argue the point, but we were going to talk to Paul on our way out. "What makes you think that?"

"She's always calling him after work, and sometimes he leaves and goes over to her apartment." Joyce and I could see that she was getting upset, so we tried to convince her not to worry about Paul and just concentrate on getting better.

After leaving the hospital, we went looking for this "easy shop" that Paul worked at. After much searching, we finally happened upon it. We filled the car up with gas and went inside. Sure enough, there he was behind the counter. Good he was alone at the time. When we walked in, he said that he knew that we were going to come by. "Okay, so you hit that nail on the head," I said. "Cut the crap, Paul. What's going on with you and Cindy, and why does she think you're seeing another woman?"

Chapter 20

Paul, the Savior

P aul started to explain, "Nancy works here, and sometimes we are on duty together. She was just getting over a nasty break up and needed a shoulder to cry on, no more no less. The guy she was dating was on drugs and refused to get help. I could relate to that, and I would tell her my experiences with drugs. She wanted him to get help, but he wouldn't and would beat her up if she didn't give him money to help support his habit. I told Nancy that he would have to want to get help on his own, and nothing she said or did would change that. I told her to get out and find someplace else to go. Nancy didn't want to go home to her mother because she didn't want her involved. So she put her stuff in storage and stayed at a motel until she found an apartment that was in her price range. Yes, I helped her move in, and I do stop by there from time to time but that's the extend of it, just friendship." If he thought we believed that cock-and-bull story, then I see that he doesn't know me and Joyce very well. Customers started coming in. So we left, not before telling him to call me after he saw Cindy.

We talked about how worried we were about our friend on the ride home. I hadn't called Sam yet and was still not sure whether I was going to or not. The more I thought about it, I figured that I better let her know something, especially with Cindy still in the hospital, and you never can tell about these things.

Calling Sam was not one of my better ideas even though she needed to know. All she heard was hospital and Cindy. Getting her to calm down and listen so that I could try to tell her what the doctor said was a chore within itself. "She should be going home tomorrow, and aren't you coming down to visit her this month? Then you will be able to see for yourself how she's doing." After a few more minutes of reassuring her, she calmed down and felt a little better. I told her to call me when she came down, and maybe I'd be able to meet her in Charlotte.

"Love you, Aunt Brett," she said. "And take care of momma until I get there."

"I will, baby, don't you worry. Love you too. Good night."

As promised, Paul called to give me an update on Cindy. The doctor said that everything looked good; and if there were no problems tonight, she will be cleared to go home tomorrow. He told me that he was taking the next couple of days off to be there for Cindy. That was great news about her being released, and I was glad that he was taking some time off to be with her. I told him to call me as soon as he got her home.

Cindy was discharged the next day. Paul picked her up and took her home as promised. She called me after she got settled in and had taken a nap. She assured me that she felt good and was going to take it easy for the rest of the day. We talked for a while until Paul got back from picking up her medicine and a few packages from the store. I didn't bring up the subject of Paul and Nancy because I didn't want her getting upset. We would have plenty of time to talk later about that.

My biggest concern right now is whether Cindy was using drugs. I knew that Paul wouldn't just come out with a yes or no answer without beating around the bush. I needed to catch him by himself and talk to him, maybe one-on-one with just me and him, and he would come clean about a lot of things. I texted him and told him to call me when he was alone and not around Cindy. He said that he would call me when he took his break at work. "Thanks," I texted.

Keeping his word, he called me like he said he would. "Paul, please tell me the truth about what's going on with you and Cindy."

He took a deep breath, and then he said, "Cindy is spinning out of control. Did you know that she quit her job so that she can come to work and watch me?"

"Why did she feel the need to do this?" I asked.

"It's because of Nancy."

"Please tell me why."

"Brett, I'm going to be honest with you. Cindy is chasing me away. She has even been trying to get me to use again. She even has Bobby, one of our drug dealer friends from St. Paul, coming up here to bring drugs. I think that she feels if she gets me using again that she would be able to keep me under her wing. I just can't do it anymore. I am trying my best to keep it together."

"Don't give up. Stay strong," I told him. "Don't, by any means, give in."

"Brett, you just don't know how hard it is."

"Well, I'll tell you what, when you feel that urge to use kicking in, call me, and we'll talk." This is how Paul and I became friends. Talking and listening to him, I was beginning to understand and see him in a different light. He would call me all the time to talk, especially when Bobby came down.

Bobby was beginning to be a problem, but Paul didn't know how to discuss it with Cindy. Everything caused her to explode and go into one of her rages. So for the most part, he would just leave it alone. I knew that this situation was about to blow up.

Sure enough, Cindy called me one night, crying because Paul had moved out. He didn't tell her where he was going, but she suspects that it was to Nancy's apartment. I called Paul and called him, but he would not pick up. "Lord, I sure don't feel like taking off a day to go up there to deal with Cindy's craziness." Cindy must have called me at least five times that night, complaining about Paul. I told her to let it go and stop worrying about him. I told her to calm down before she made herself sick. That only made her angrier. I was tired and wanted her to go to sleep.

The phone rang and rang. Without looking at it, I felt that it was Cindy. I didn't answer it because I didn't feel like hearing anymore drama tonight. The phone began to ring again. This time, I picked it up, not knowing what I would be listening to this time.

"Hello, Brett, it's Paul," he said.

"Paul, excuse my French, but what in the hell is going on with you and Cindy?" I questioned.

"Brett, I just couldn't take any more!" he screamed.

"Okay, calm down. Where are you?" I asked.

He got quiet for a minute, and then he finally answered, "I'm at Nancy's place."

"You no good son—" Before I could say anymore, he cut me off.

"It's not like that, Brett. I'm just crashing her tonight. I need to think. I couldn't stay at the apartment tonight. Bobby and a few of his friends were there ready to party and get high. I had to get out. I tried talking to Cindy, but she wasn't hearing anything that I had to say. I tried to reach Reverend Jamison, but I didn't get an answer. I'm staying here tonight and will stay with Reverend Jamison for a few days until I can talk to Cindy."

"Okay, we will talk tomorrow about what happened between the two of you. Now you know that I had to call Joyce to tell her what happened."

"That no good son of a bitch," she said.

"Let's get ready to go up there Saturday morning and see if we can make some sense out of this mess. In the meantime, I'll call you from work tomorrow because I am sleepy, and I am going to sleep now. Night, night."

That Friday, during a midmorning break, I could barely talk for being so upset with Cindy and Paul. I knew that in my heart of hearts, Cindy was going to do something stupid. I had been trying to reach her all morning, but she is mad with me and not answering my calls. Finally right before I was getting ready to leave work at five, she called me and told me that she had handled her business and hung up the phone. Oh Lord, what has this fool done! My mind was racing a mile a minute. I called her back as fast as I could. "Pick up, pick up." I kept saying to myself over and over, but it went straight to voice mail. At the time, I didn't think about calling Paul, so I called Joyce instead. Joyce picked up as soon as her phone rang. "Joyce, Joyce," I yelled. "I just got the weirdest call from Cindy. She said, 'I handled my business.' And hung up."

"What the hell was she talking about?"

"I don't know. That's all she said."

"You don't think that she tried to kill Paul?"

"I don't know, Joyce, and she won't answer the phone."

"Did you call Paul?"

"No, I'm scared."

"Girl, go on and call the man. If he's dead, he won't answer," she said laughing. I called her an asshole and hung up. Nervously I dialed Paul's number, holding my breath and praying. No answer, so I hung up and dialed again, no answer.

This time, I let it go to voice mail. "Paul, this is Brett. Please give me a call as soon as you get this message."

I called Joyce. She picked up the phone laughing. "Did he answer?"

"No," I said.

She yells out laughing, "Cindy done killed Paul!"

"Bye fool," I said and hung up. I had to chuckle to myself.

I could not sleep that night at all. I was on pins and needles worrying about Cindy. Around 1:00 a.m., the phone rang, and it was Paul. "Paul, I am glad to hear your voice. What's going on with Cindy?"

"Brett, I just don't know what to do. This morning, when I got to work, Cindy was already there, sitting in the parking lot. Nancy dropped me off and left. I walked to the store's door to unlock it and go in. By this time, Cindy had gotten out of her car and walked to the door, so I held it open so she could walk in. I went to clock in, and she took a seat in one of the booths. When I came out, she came where I was and started talking about us and how we need to fix our situation. I told her that I cared about her, but I needed space to get my head on right and that I can't be hanging around her as long as she has Bobby and his friends coming to the apartment all the time.

Cindy hadn't heard a word that I had said because the next thing she asked, 'Do you need money?' She repeated what she said, 'You need money. And this time she started pulling these bills out of her purse and throwing them on the counter. I told her to put the money back in her purse and go home, that I would come by later and talk to her." He said around the time he was supposed to get off, she came back to the store and sat in her car for a minute or so. Then she got out and came in. "She walked in, smiled at me, and walked over to the coffee machine and made herself a large cup of cappuccino and sat, now sipping on it. She got up and walked over to the counter, looked at me, smiled, and threw the coffee in my face and ran out the store. It just happened so fast. The other guy had gotten in about five minutes ago and was in the back, clocking in and putting his things into his locker. When he heard me screaming, he came running to see what was wrong. He saw me doubled over with the hot coffee dripping from my face and called 911. They came and tried to treat me there but took me to the hospital because it went in my eyes. They wanted to make sure that there was no damage done to them. I have minor burns on my face and arms I'm just glad that it didn't harm my eyes. They gave me something for the pain and told me to take it easy for a day or two."

"I'm glad that it wasn't any worse than it is. Do you know where Cindy is?" I asked.

"I don't know. And right now, I don't give a damn where the hell she is."

"So, what are you going to do?"

"I had one of the nurses call Reverend Jamison, and he is on his way to pick me up. I am going to stay with him for a while until I can figure out what to do about Cindy."

"Okay, I'll check on you tomorrow. And Paul for what it's worth, I am sorry about what Cindy did."

"It's not your fault, Brett. Take care."

I waited until morning to call Joyce and give her a recap of the events of last night. She could not believe what I told her Paul said happened. She kept repeating, "You are kidding. You are kidding."

"Brett," she finally asked, "do you think that she has stopped taking her meds again?"

"Joyce, that crossed my mind, but I don't know. I just don't know." We were hoping that she didn't go off the deep end again and disappear not letting anyone know where she is.

In the meantime, I kept calling and calling, but she would not answer her phone. I even called Nathan to let him know what was going on, thinking that she might have called him. I told him that I hadn't contacted Sam to let her know. He said, "Good, let's keep it like that for the time being. If it gets to a point where we need to contact Sam, I'll handle it." He also told me not to worry, that if I didn't hear from her in the next couple days, he would find her.

Remembering that I told Paul that I would call and check on him today, I dialed his number. His phone rang a couple of times before he answered, "Hello, Brett."

"Hello, how are you feeling today?" I asked.

"Better than yesterday." He laughed. "I'm still in a little pain, but I'll survive."

"I am so glad to hear that." Then I asked him had he heard from Cindy.

"No and the two of us really need to talk."

"Yeah, you are so right. So what do you think that you are going to do?"

"First, let me say this. The store wants me to press charges against her, but I told them that I was all right, and I'm not going to do that. Since I won't press charges, they are banning her from the store. If she comes there again, she will be arrested."

"I can understand that."

"Brett, do you have a minute?"

"Sure," I said.

"Brett, I have known for some time that I needed to move away from Cindy. She has changed since we first started knowing each other. She is becoming too needy. She is expecting too much from me right now. I'm just getting to a point where I'm learning how to take care of me. I keep trying to tell her that, but she either doesn't listen, care, or understand. Then with her bringing Bobby around was the last straw. I think that Cindy forgets that I am a recovering drug addict, and I don't need to be in that environment. Cindy means the world to me, but how can she expect me to give her love when I don't even know how to love myself. She thought that giving me drugs and money was what I needed to stay there with her, but this is what was chasing me away." I completely understood where he was coming from. It was beginning to make a lot of sense now. Cindy was trying to control him by getting him back on drugs, typical Cindy move. Well, I am glad that he stood strong and fought it. Then Paul asked me had I heard from Cindy. I told him no and that I was hoping that she had tried to contact him. This did not make me feel any better. No one knew where she was. Paul and I talked some more until his pain medicine started kicking in, and he was beginning to get drowsy. I told him that I would talk to him later and hung up.

After telling Joyce about our conversation, Chris and I decided to watch a movie. Just as the movie started getting interesting, my phone rang. At first, I started not to answer it, but it kept ringing. Reaching for the phone, I could see that it was Cindy. "Hello, hello," I said. "Cindy, where are you?"

"Don't worry about where the fuck I am, bitch. Just know that I handled my business!" Then she hung up the phone. I called her back immediately, but she would not answer that phone. Chris, seeing that I was upset, told me to give it a rest. She'll call back when she's ready to talk. I knew or at least I hoped he was right and went back to looking at the movie. I could not concentrate no matter how hard I tried because I knew that Cindy was in a crisis.

The next night, around 9:00, Cindy started calling me. She was cussing me and Joyce out left and right. We were no good bitches and didn't give a damn about her. When I tried to say something, she hung up. This went on until about two in the morning. Cindy must have called me about thirty or more times; but if I called her back, she would not answer the phone. I didn't want to turn my phone off just in case she would stop cussing me long enough to talk. Well, that didn't happen, but the calls did stop until about six o'clock the next morning. Cindy called, crying and apologizing for how she was acting last night. "No problem, Cindy, but are you all right and where are you?"

"Right now, I'm in Charlotte at the apartment."

"Is Paul there?"

"No, I don't know where he is. He wasn't at work last night, and he wasn't at Nancy's. So I don't know where he is. Brett, I think that I really messed things up with Paul this time."

"What did you do to make you think like that?" I asked her.

"Remember when I told you that I handled my business?"

"Yeah, what did that mean?"

"Well, I got tired of him cheating on me with that whore Nancy, so I went to the store the other night and threw hot coffee in his fucking face."

"Cindy, I'm going to be honest with you. I heard about that. But why throw coffee in his face? You could have damaged his eyes."

She yelled, "What the fuck I care about that no-good son of a bitch! I'm through with his sorry ass anyway."

"So what are you going to do now? I don't know. And right now, I don't care."

"Why don't you go visit Sam for a while? I'm sure that she would be glad to see you."

"You know what, Brett, I might just do that. A break from around here might do me a world of good." Hallelujah, something she agreed with. That would save Sam the trip that she was going to make to see her in Charlotte.

She called Sam and told her about her plans to come and visit her. Sam was out of her mind with excitement. She called me immediately after talking to her mother to tell me the news. "Great news, Sam. I'm sure that she is going to enjoy herself." Her plans were to stay with Sam for two weeks. But remember, we are talking about Cindy. It could be shorter or longer. Cindy left the very next day.

Sam picked her up from the airport and called to let me know that she had made it there safe and sound. "Good, Sam, we'll talk later. In the meantime, enjoy your visit with your mom. Tell Cindy that I will call her in a day or two."

Cindy had been gone about three days; and before I could call Sam or Cindy, Sam called me upset. "Aunt Brett," she whispered over the phone, "something is wrong with Momma. She's not physically sick, but there is something not right. She's jumpy and moody. Sometimes at night, I hear her crying in the room. Is something going on that I need to know about?"

"No, she and Paul are going through a rough patch. She probably just misses him. Tell her to give me a call later today."

I never did hear from Cindy, so I called her. But she didn't answer the phone. I called her several times that day, but she never would answer the phone. I didn't call anymore, and I didn't want to worry Sam because I didn't know what Cindy had said to her. Knowing Cindy, she probably had Sam thinking that we had been talking all the time. The next thing I knew, Cindy was on a plane, coming back to Charlotte from Sam's home in Maryland.

What is she up to? I wondered. Joyce called me later that day. I told her what was going on with Cindy. We tried to put our heads together to figure out what she was up to and what her next move would be. I called Paul to see if he had heard from her since she had gotten back in town. "Not a word," he said.

"Okay," I said. "Just be on the lookout and let me know if you see or hear from her."

Chapter 21

The Reverend Jamison

D ays passed, and we hadn't heard anything from Cindy. Joyce and I decided to take a trip to Charlotte to see if we could make contact with Cindy. We went to the apartment, and her car wasn't there. So we called Paul and asked where he was. He was off that day and was at Reverend Jamison's house. He gave us the address and directions and told us to come to there. He wanted us to meet Reverend Jamison, and I was anxious to meet him too since I had heard so much about him from Cindy and Paul.

It didn't take us long to find Reverend Jamison's house. The neighborhood where he lived seemed to be in a nice area of town. When we pulled into the driveway, Paul came out to meet us. We stopped, got out of the car, and walked to meet Paul. He hugged us and invited us to come inside. The home was exquisite inside. I thought that I was standing in a segment of *Life Styles of the Rich and Famous*. Reverend and Mrs. Jamison came out to meet us and welcome us to their home. Joyce and I told them how beautiful their home was. We followed them to the family room where they thought that we would be more comfortable. The view from the room was breathtaking. Just sitting there would make any blah day bright again. I could understand why Paul liked staying there. The five of us talked for over two hours like we had known each other for ages. Reverend Jamison was very insightful into what Joyce and I were going through with Cindy. He said that in a sense, we were letting Cindy control us.

At first, Joyce and I didn't see or understand what he meant. As we talked more about it, we could see that he was right. Cindy had us dangling like puppets on a string. We don't hear from her, and we go into a *panic* and start looking for her. She calls crying, and we go into a *panic* and go looking for her. It was becoming an endless cycle with Cindy controlling the strings. He was right. We would fall into her trap every time. Instead of us ignoring her and letting her reach out to us, we were rescuing her from herself. In actuality, she is crying out for help. That was why she couldn't fathom Paul not depending on her anymore. She saw him as being in worst shape than her. She was trying to "self-cure" by helping Paul. In her mind, if she was able to help him than she wasn't as bad off as she felt. That's why she tried to get him back on drugs so that he would need her. Reverend Jamison said, "I hate to say this about Cindy, but she is a ticking time bomb. And she needs help fast."

Mrs. Jamison fixed us a fantastic meal of fried chicken, macaroni and cheese, mustard greens, and cornbread. It was very tasty. After dinner, we talked for a bit more until we realized how late it was getting, and we knew that we needed to get on the road. Joyce and I said our goodbyes and made promises that we would keep in touch.

On the trip home, Joyce and I had a lot to talk about. First and foremost, we had to find Cindy before she did something else to Paul. We knew in our hearts that she was not through with him. Before leaving, we warned him to be careful and be on the lookout for Cindy. We had a feeling that she was still in the Charlotte area and that she was watching Paul's every move. Knowing her, she probably switched cars with someone so that she could follow him without being recognized. I asked Joyce if she thought that it was time to involve Sam. I decided to wait, but I would talk to Nathan to get his take on the situation. It was fact facing time. We had to find Cindy and get her into therapy before she hurt herself or did harm to someone else.

I called Nathan and told him that I needed to talk with him about something important. He knew that this meant it had something to do with Cindy. He came over to my job that Tuesday. He knew that she had been to visit their daughter, Sam, and had left after a few days. "I didn't want to call Sam, but do you know if she has heard from Cindy since she's been back?" He said that she didn't mention anything when he talked to her on Sunday.

I told him what Reverend Jamison said about Cindy and controlling us through these mind games of hers. Nathan said, "You know that Cindy likes to be in control and have her way no matter at what cost."

"Yeah, you're right." I said. But we still didn't know where the heck Cindy was.

He said, "Give it a few more days, and she will contact one of us." I knew that he was right, but I couldn't help worrying about her.

Chapter 22

The Waiting Game

Playing the waiting game was no fun at all. Nathan, Joyce, and I tried reaching out to her when we hadn't heard from her by the end of the week. Nathan tried tracking her down and found her car. She had switched cars with a former student and was using her car. Nathan got the make and model of the car and the tag number. One of his law-enforcement buddies was able to trace the car to the parking lot of where Paul worked. She was still following him; but since she wasn't allowed on the premises, she would put on a wig and go in her former student Sherry's car. What was she waiting to do to Paul this time? Nathan told me to call and tell Paul what was happening and to stay away from her for the time being. Nathan got in touch with Bobby to find out if he knew what going on with Cindy. He swore up and down that he hadn't been in touch with her in about two weeks, but he heard on the street that she was trying to get a gun. Now we didn't know if she got the gun or not. Nathan knew the guy that Bobby said they sent her to. Nathan went to talk to him and asked him if he had sold Cindy a gun. He said that he didn't sell her a gun because she never came to him. Nathan knew that Cindy was smart enough that she would send someone else to get it for her. This time, Nathan called Paul himself and explained to him what he suspected. He told him that if he could, take a few days off from work and lie low. He told Paul that he would call him later. "Thanks man," he said.

Nathan called me to let me know that he was going to Charlotte to get Cindy. I wanted to go with him, but he told me no because he didn't know what he was walking into. It's rumored that she might have a gun. "Be careful, Nathan. Please call me and let me know what happens."

I went to Joyce's house to wait to hear from Nathan. Sitting there, we tried not to think about it, but we were on pins and needles waiting to hear from Nathan. Finally he called. He had found Cindy; and sure enough, she had a gun. He got it away from her without incident, but she was in a mess. He was bringing her to St. Paul, and we told him to bring her to Joyce's house.

We were sitting in the window, talking and looking for Nathan's car. When we saw his car turn the corner, we jumped up and ran out to the driveway. He pulled in and stopped. We ran around to Cindy's side of the car, opened the door, and helped Cindy out. At first, she jerked away from us and walked past us into the house and slammed the door in our faces. I stayed behind to talk with Nathan. He said that she is really in bad shape and needs to go to a doctor. "Good luck with that," he said.

"Are you coming in," I asked.

"No, let me go, so I can get rid of this gun." I just shook my head and walked away. "I'll see you later," he said.

"Okay, talk to you later."

When I went inside, Joyce was trying to have a conversation with Cindy which looked like it was one-sided. I wondered if Cindy had been taking her medicine and looked in her pocketbook to see if they were in there. Just as I thought, she hadn't been taking her meds. Therefore, that explained why her behavior was so erratic, that with the fact that she needed to go to therapy. I got a glass of water and made her take her meds. We made her lie down on one of the beds to rest and give the meds a chance to work.

Joyce and I went back in the den to talk. I told her that Nathan said that she did have a gun. He found her in Sherry's car just sitting in the parking lot. She was wearing a disguise. She had on a brown wig and dark shades. He said that it was a good thing that he told

Paul to take a couple of days off from work because there was no telling how this would have played out.

Nathan called later to check on Cindy. Joyce told him that we had given her meds and made her lie down. She was still sleeping. She told him that we would call him when she woke up. The next question, "Who's going to tell Sam?" I told Joyce that I thought that Nathan should be the one to talk with her about Cindy so that he could help her decide what to do about helping her.

Cindy was awake and came into the den. "Bitches, what y'all doing in here?"

"Oh, so you finally decided to wake up. I was getting ready to come in there and put a mirror to your nose," I joked. "How you feeling?"

"Great!" she replied. "Okay, go ahead and ask. I know that the two of you are dying to know the details of what happened and what's going on."

"We are, so spill the tea."

Paul had been cheating on me with this bitch named Nancy. I would catch him talking to her on the phone all the time, and he never would tell me what they were talking about. At the store, she was always there even when she wasn't working. I got fed up and asked him what the fuck was going on. He would lie and say nothing. "We are just friends. She's having problems with her boyfriend and needs a shoulder to cry on."

"BULLSHIT!" she yelled. "He's fucking that damn bitch and ain't got the balls to admit it." Maybe it's just that I said, knowing that I was opening up a can of whip ass. "Shut the fuck up, Brett," which I politely did without being told a second time.

Joyce looked at me, laughed, and whispered, "I bet you'll keep your damn mouth shut now."

"Anyway, as I was saying, he thought that he was getting over on me, but I showed his ass. I was watching him, and he didn't even know it. He even stayed at the bitch's house one night. I wasn't having that. Ain't no telling what dick she done had up in that stink ass pussy!" Joyce and I looked at each other, knowing not to say a word. We sat in complete silence and listened as she went on with her tirade. "That's all right though. I handled my business! I bet he was singing a different tune when that hot coffee hit his damn face."

So Joyce did talk then, "They could have locked your ass up! What were you thinking?"

"He better be glad that I didn't shoot his ass."

"So what are you going to do now?"

"Pack up and move my black ass back to St. Paul."

"What about Paul?"

"What the fuck do you mean 'what about Paul?' He needs to go and get his shit out of the apartment, or I'm going to put them in the trash."

"Do you want me to call and tell him?"

"Brett, that's up to you. I don't give a fuck."

In all the excitement, I forgot to call Nathan to let him know that she was awake and back to her old self. "Cindy, I'll call you when I get home." The first call I made was to Paul. I told him that Cindy was in St. Paul and plans to give the apartment up and move back home. He said that they had four more months on the lease without losing the deposit. "Okay, I'll tell her that. But in the meantime, you might need to start getting your things out of the apartment."

"Brett, can I talk to Cindy?"

"Paul, I don't think that is a good idea at the moment. Give her a day or two. Then call her. I'm not making any promises that she will talk to you, but you can try."

"Brett, do you mind if I call you later to just talk?"

"Sure, that will be fine."

Joyce took Cindy home and made sure that she had everything she needed. We told her that we would go with her Wednesday to help her pack up the apartment and pick up her car. Well, she couldn't wait and went to Charlotte the next day. Getting a car in St. Paul was not a problem for her. Any number of people would gladly let her borrow their car. I called Paul and told him to be on the look-out because we think that Cindy was on the way to Charlotte.

Here we go again, waiting to hear from Cindy. Then we realized that she was a grown woman, and we couldn't spend our lives worrying about her. We were letting Cindy and her problems consume us. I called Nathan and told him that he needed to talk with Sam immediately about getting her some type of help. He said that he would call Sam and ask her to come down so that they could set up an appointment to take her to see a doctor. Cindy did come back that night. She didn't see Paul because he still hadn't gone back to work, but he told me when he called later that night that he had transferred to another store. He was renting an apartment from a friend of Reverend Jamison. Everything was going good, but he was still worried about Cindy. Give her time, just give her time.

Chapter 23

Getting Cindy Help

S am got here the following week. She went to the house where her mom was. She told Cindy that she didn't like the way she was acting when she came to visit her and that her and dad were concerned about her health and wanted her to go to counseling. She was not hearing that. Sam started to cry and told her that she didn't want her to end up like Grand momma. Cindy started remembering her mother and how sick she had become and began to cry. Sam went on to tell her that she wanted her children to know their grandmother and she needs her in her life. Hearing the sincerity in Sam's voice made Cindy agree to go and see a doctor.

Sam made the appointment for the following day after their talk. They went to a different one from the one they took Mrs. Smalls to. This was the only condition of her agreeing to go to the doctor. So they went to see Dr. Glenn in Raleigh, North Carolina. Sam said that Dr. Glenn had a long one-on-one with Cindy. When Sam spoke with him, he wouldn't divulge anything that Cindy had told him in the strictest of confidence. As with Mrs. Smalls, he wanted to admit her for in-house treatment for two weeks, then weekly sessions. He really wanted to keep her longer, but she would not agree to that. It was either two weeks or none. Knowing that she desperately needed treatment, he took what he could get. Dr. Glenn was also hoping that he would be able to get her to commit to staying longer. Boy, he sure didn't know Cindy. Leaving Cindy that day at the facilities was one of the hardest things Sam had to do. She called me on her way back to St. Paul to tell me what happened and asked me to meet her at the house to help her pack a bag for Cindy.

Sam was going to take the bag to the hospital and leave it with the nurse. Then she was headed back home to Maryland. The two weeks that Cindy was away were hard because we could not communicate with her. Dr. Glenn would give Sam updates as to how the treatments were going. I went with Sam so that I could take her to the airport. Sam was in tears when she came out of the hospital. It's a good thing that the airport wasn't far from the hospital because it was a quiet ride. It was so quiet as my daddy used to say, "You could hear a rat pee on cotton." Sam didn't want to leave her momma, but she knew that this was for the best. I gave her lots of hugs and kisses and reminded her that her daddy and I were just a phone call away. As she walked away, she stopped and looked at me and said, "Aunt Brett, please take care of my momma."

"Of course, I will. Don't you worry. Call me when you get home. Love you."

The long ride home gave me a chance to reflect and remember the old Cindy. My mind went back to the time when she was dating Lenell and Brad at the same time. There was a time when Cindy started gaining weight, stomach stayed upset, and she was moodier than usual even for her. Jokingly I said, "Girl, is you done got yourself knocked up?"

She got this strange look on her face and said, "I hope the hell not!" She went by the drugstore on her way home and got a pregnancy test. Cindy called me later that night to tell me that she had peed on the little stick, and it was positive.

"When are you going to tell Lenell?"

"Never," she replied. He will never know about this baby. I thought that was strange, but I kept my mouth closed. I asked her what she was going to do.

She said, "Get rid of it. I'm going to make the arrangements, and I need you to go with me." Now, I wasn't too sure about that and talked it over with my mother. She told me that I shouldn't go, but I was between being sensible and being loyal. Loyalty won, and

I told her that I would go. I often wondered if Cindy didn't tell Lenell because she felt that the baby was Brad's. Well, only Cindy knew, and that was something she would take to the grave with her. I don't know what made me think of that. I guess my mind was just wandering.

I could feel Cindy slipping away from me, and it scared me to death because there was nothing that I could do. Thinking about the good and the bad, I cried and laughed all the way home. It was going to be a long two weeks without being able to talk to Cindy. Yeah, I know. This wouldn't be the first time that I had gone this long without talking to Cindy, but this time was different. I can't explain how, but it was just different.

Sam would call me every day after she talked with Dr. Glenn to give me an update on how Cindy was progressing. It was a slow battle uphill, and right now he was doing all the work. Dr. Glenn said that she was in a dark place, and it's as if she has locked herself in and thrown away the key. Sam said that Dr. Glenn asked her if she or Nathan knew of anything that happened in her past that would put her in this state. There was nothing that stood out in either one of their minds. I said to myself that I could think of a few things that I picked up on from conversations with Cindy and from listening to idle gossip. But I didn't feel that it was my place to say anything; and who knows in the long run, it might have made things worse.

At the end of the two weeks, Cindy left and came back to St. Paul. No one knew that she had been in a mental institution and just assumed that she was with her daughter Sam. To keep her from traveling so far, Dr. Glenn made arrangements for Cindy to meet with a colleague of his in Logan three times a week. Dr. Glenn would see her in six months unless his colleague felt otherwise. We were so proud of Cindy because she was keeping her appointments and seemed to be doing great.

Come to find out it was too good to be true. Cindy kept her appointments for the first week. The next week, she would go to the office, sign in and leave. The weeks to follow were more of the same. She had Sam, Nathan, and the rest of us thinking that she was at therapy, but she was spending her days at the apartment in Charlotte.

Dr. Glenn told Sam that this was a waste of time and money because Cindy wasn't taking the treatments seriously. In tears, Sam asked Dr. Glenn what to do. He said, "At the present, honestly, I don't know. In order for the therapy to work, she has got to want to do it. She's been playing a game from the very beginning. She's a great manipulator which makes her a danger to herself and others right now. Cindy needs to get rid of the apartment in Charlotte." Dr. Glenn suggested that she call the manager of the apartment and explain to them the circumstances of her needing to leave before her lease is up, and they might let you break the lease. I'll fax a letter to them telling them that she is a patient of mine and does not need to be staying there alone at this time. They granted the request and even returned the deposit. Sam asked me and Joyce to go and take her things out of the apartment. Nathan said that he would go with us just to be on the safe side.

When we arrived at the apartment complex, we stopped by the office to let them know that we were there. The manager went with us to open the door and let us in. Cindy had everything packed up and sitting in the middle of the living room floor. I called Paul to tell him that we were moving the things out of the apartment and that he needed to come and get his stuff if he hadn't already. He kind of hesitated at first until I told him who was here with me. He hung up and came right over. After he got his things, he helped Nathan load the heavy items into the truck. With him helping, we were finished and on our way back to St. Paul. Before leaving, Paul wanted to know how Cindy was doing. I kind of shook my head and said not well. Looking at the ground, he said that he blamed himself for Cindy and her behavior. I asked him, "Why? Did something happen that we should know about?"

He said, "Nothing in particular, I just feel that I should have stuck by her instead of leaving, but I'm a recovering drug addict. And I just couldn't deal with some of the shit that Cindy was going through. All I needed was a little space and time to get my head on right. Oh, Brett, I'm so sorry. I am so sorry."

"It's okay, just as long as we learn from our mistakes." I hugged him and told him to keep in touch.

It's a good thing we rode with Nathan in that big Ford truck of his because I was exhausted and slept all the way to St. Paul. We put Cindy's things in a storage shed that Nathan had at his house. The three of us talked for a minute, and then Joyce and I were on our way. I didn't even go in at Joyce's house because I was tired and ready to get back to Logan. As soon as I walked in the door at my house, I called Cindy; and to my surprise, she answered the phone.

"I see that y'all got my shit to St. Paul in one piece. You were out there, weren't you?"

"I thought that I saw you pass by, but I didn't say anything to the rest of them. Where are you?

"Oh, here and there," she said.

"How are you feeling?"

"Great!"

"Why don't you come to Logan for a while?"

"HELL NO! You all are just trying to set a trap for me."

"Why would you think that? No one is trying to trap you. We are all just concerned about you."

"You're a lying bitch," she said and hung up. I called her back several times. She would answer the phone; and when I started to talk, she would call me a bitch and hang up the phone. I called Joyce and told her what was going on, so she said that she would call her.

Joyce called me back and said that whore had the nerve to call me a bitch and hang up the damn phone. "What is wrong with her?"

Paul called me that night and said that Cindy had called him and wanted to see him. He told her that he didn't think that was a good idea after what happened the last time they saw each other. He told her that he would have to think about it and call her back. He hung up from her and immediately called Reverend Jamison. He told him about Cindy wanting to meet him, but that he was a little uneasy about meeting her alone. Reverend Jamison suggested that they meet at the church. He would be there, and I'm sure that she wouldn't try something there. "Tell her to meet you at the church, 11:00, Thursday morning. I will be meeting with some of the deacons there at that time." Paul called her back and told her where to come and that he would meet her there at 11:00 a.m. Thursday.

Lord, I pray that everything would go all right on Thursday. Hopefully Cindy would take her crazy medicine and would be in somewhat of a good frame of mind. I know. I know. I made a promise that I was not going to get caught up in Cindy's drama. Somehow I was beginning to find out that it was easier said than done. I just had to pray harder about it and let it go.

Paul called me early Thursday morning. He was kind of anxious about seeing Cindy. He asked me did I have any words of wisdom. We both laughed, and then I said, "Say a prayer because you are going to need all the help that you can get." He laughed, but I was serious. "Call me after you meet with her."

Chapter 24

The Meeting

Cindy showed up on time and was met by Reverend Jamison. At least she knew that there were others in the church just in case she wanted to show her behind. Paul showed up a few minutes later; and when he saw Cindy, he walked over and embraced her. Reverend Jamison was still there and told them that they could use his office to talk. He told them that if they needed anything, he would be next door in the conference room.

They walked silently into Reverend Jamison's office and closed the door. It was awkward at first because neither one knew what to say, but Cindy broke the ice and asked him why.

"What do you mean?"

"Why did you leave me and treated me the way that you did? If something was wrong, then we should have been able to talk about it. But instead you shut me out."

"I didn't mean to, but I didn't know how to talk about my feelings without making you upset. So I ran. I realize now that I was wrong. I just found it easy to talk to Nancy because I didn't have a connection with her. There was never anything between us... nothing...nothing at all. Her boyfriend is on drugs, and I could relate to what he was putting her through. The night I stayed at her apartment, we talked most of the night. Or at least she talked, and I listened. When we finally went to sleep, I slept on the couch fully dressed. There was never anything sexual between us. Cindy, you must understand I had been on drugs for years. During that time, I didn't have to think about anything or anyone. The only thing that was on my mind was where I was going to get my next fix from and how I was going to pay for it. I did not care about nothing. And I'm ashamed to say this, but I didn't even think about you. Yes, I cared about you, but my need for drugs trumped everything and anything, including you. That's why it was so easy for me to trade your car for drugs, but something made me realize that I had done something wrong and that I needed to leave. The Lord must have been with me to lead me to Reverend Jamison. I will always be grateful to him for pointing me in the right direction. Him helping me to get into treatment was a new beginning for me. I saw my shortcomings and began to work on them. Through therapy, I learned that I needed to be able to love myself before I could love someone else. I know that I told you that I loved you, but I didn't know what love was. I was just going through the motions, telling you what I thought you wanted to hear. I didn't give a damn whether it was true or not. It took me almost dying to realize that my life mattered. I owe my life to Reverend Jamison for helping me to get and stay on the right track. Cindy, I really feel good about myself."

"I finally realize what it is to love me, Paul. Now I am able to be there for you. I want you back in my life because I love you!" Cindy started to cry as Paul walked over and embraced her. Is this what Cindy needs right now? Was Paul being sincere? Tune in to find out. Whether it was true or not, Cindy swallowed it hook, line, and sinker. The rest of the time at the church, they spend talking and planning their future. They would stay in Paul's apartment for now until they decided if they wanted to stay in Charlotte or move somewhere else.

After the reverend's meeting, he joined Cindy and Paul in his office where the two of them told him about their plans. He was overjoyed for them, as well as a little apprehensive. Is this really what the two of them needed? Giving them the benefit of the doubt, he gave them his blessings and told them that his doors were always open day or night.

They thanked him and went to one of the local restaurants to get something to eat. Cindy stayed in Charlotte with Paul that night but came back the next day to get some of her belongings. She called me while she was at home. I must admit that she sounded like the old Cindy. She was in high spirits as we talked. She said, "Things are going to be okay. Don't you worry."

I said, "I'll try not to while crossing my fingers and saying a little prayer. Call me when you get settled."

"I will."

True to her word, she called me as soon as she got in. We talked for a minute or so because Paul was at work. I asked her again if this is what she wanted to do. She assured me that it was 100 percent what she wanted. I didn't bring it up anymore. I told her that if she was happy, then I was happy for her. "I am," she said. That was the end of that.

Needless to say, that was the end of her therapy sessions also. There was no need in trying to get her to go back. Sam tried but gave up when she realized that her mother was getting ready to shut down and not let anyone in, so she said, "To hell with it."

Things were going great with her and Paul for a while; but as I said before, commitment scares Cindy. So she started getting itchy and went looking for Robert, her security blanket. He played along and talked about her around the clubs where he would be working. She was buying him things and giving him money. Robert really irked me, the way he was laughing and talking about her behind her back. I caught up with Robert and told him that he was wrong for what he was doing and saying about Cindy. Well, when Joyce got wind of it, she went straight to Cindy with it. She was furious! She had been hearing bits and pieces, but she thought that they were just messing around. Lord, forbid if this got back to Paul. Since Robert wanted to play dirty, she decided to do the same thing. She called Brenda and told her everything about all his women and all his baby mamas, especially about his special baby mama, Betty. Brenda couldn't believe what she was hearing. Robert had promised her that he was through with all of them, but what she heard that shocked her was the relationship between him and Betty. Brenda knew Betty and had seen her at several family gatherings but thought nothing of it. Well, Brenda went to Betty's house and demanded that she stop seeing her man. Betty looked at her like she had lost her mind. "What do you mean your man? I know more about Robert than you will ever know."

Then Brenda yells, "We are engaged and I'm going to marry him."

"Over my dead body," Betty snickered. After the first of many encounters with Betty, Brenda decided to take a break from Robert. She even tried to connect with Cindy. At first, Cindy was skeptical about her but trying to make up for how she had treated her in the past. She took baby steps with forging a friendship with her. I don't think either one of them fully trusted the other one, but they knew each other's history. As time went on, they became close again.

In time, Brenda started dating Charles, a friend from work. She enjoyed being with him, and she was enjoying a drama-free relationship. Cindy was still living in Charlotte, and she and Paul seemed to be getting along well together. Brenda and Charles would visit Cindy and Paul and would double date from time to time. They both seemed to be happy.

Robert, at first, thought that it was a joke because no woman in her right mind would leave him to be with another man, especially not Brenda. Robert couldn't take it anymore. He began calling Brenda, sending her flowers and inviting her out to dinner. At first, she ignored the calls, flowers, and invites to dinner. Then she began to realize that she missed Robert because she had never stopped loving him, but she held out a little longer. She broke things off with Charles but still led Robert to believe that they were still seeing each other. Finally not being able to take it one minute more, he went to Brenda and declared his undying love for her. Then he dropped to one knee and asked her to marry him. Didn't see that coming either, did you? Of course, Brenda said yes.

Chapter 25

The Wedding

She had gotten her Robert. Hope she doesn't believe in long engagements. Brenda called Cindy before she called her mother. She told Cindy that their plan had worked. Didn't see that coming either, did you? "Robert asked me to marry him!" Brenda and Cindy had a good laugh, and then the two of them got together to celebrate. When Cindy told me and Joyce what happened, we laughed so hard that we cried! My poor cousin got played.

Brenda started planning her wedding immediately! Under much criticism, she asked Cindy to be her matron of honor. "Of course, I'd be glad to," she gleamed. It was August; and since I decided to retire, I had a lot of time on my hands. Robert suggested to Brenda to ask me to help her with the wedding.

Much to my surprise, she did ask me, and I said, "Why not, I'd love to." Brenda wanted a "New Year's eve" wedding, so we didn't have a whole lot of time to waste. She chose to have six bridesmaids, and Robert picked RJ to be his best man. RJ was excited to put it mildly. Things were falling into place nicely. Only one problem, Robert's mother didn't like Brenda and said that she wasn't going to the wedding. I knew what was going to come next.

They were going to call my momma to see if she could talk Dell into going to the wedding. Sure enough, Robert called momma and told her the situation with Dell. "Please, will you talk to her. I know that she will listen to you." Momma said that she would see what she could do. Momma told Robert to tell Dell to call her.

In a day or two, Dell called Momma. When Momma answered the phone, Dell said, "Ma, I'm not going to the wedding."

Momma said, "Hello, to you too." Dell had to laugh.

"Ma, I'm sorry, but I'm not going to that wedding. That girl Robert is marrying treat me like dirt. She acts like she don't know me." Momma listened to Dell rant and rave for a good ten minutes.

Then momma said to her, "You are going for your son."

"You're right, but he shouldn't let her treat me the way she does."

"What does she do to you, Dell?" Momma asked.

"It's just a whole lot of little things. I can ask her to help me pay a bill, and she won't give no money to help me."

Momma told her that "in the first place, you shouldn't be asking her for money to help you pay a bill. That needs to come from Robert."

"Well, I guess you're right, Ma."

"Stop acting like a child and go support your son. I will expect to see you there with bells on."

"Okay, Ma." She laughed.

Preparations were on the way for the wedding of the century. Every chance she got, she made sure Robert's baby mamas knew that she was taking Robert off the market. The wedding would be held at St. Paul United Methodist Church. Cindy and I decided to give her a bridal shower. It would be a small one with her closest friends and family. We had it one Saturday at one of the event centers in Logan. The decorations were glorious. Cindy and I outdid ourselves, with the help of Joyce of course. It had an "evening in wonderland" theme. We had the servers dressed as adult characters from *Alice in Wonderland*, serving the hors d'oeuvres. Everyone had a blast! It was a miscellaneous shower, so Brenda received a variety of nice things. She was pleased to say the least. Robert met her after the shower to help take the gifts to the car. I think that he was surprised at all the things that she had gotten.

From that day on, it was plan, plan, and plan! I was there to help as much as possible. It's a good thing that I am a fan of David

Tutera. I must admit that it was fun seeing how everything was coming together. Joyce, Cindy, and I did the rehearsal dinner for Robert. It was delicious. We did an excellent job, and everyone enjoyed it.

The day of the wedding was a beautiful day. It was as if Brenda and Robert specially ordered the day. The weather was perfect. Brenda was a vision of beauty in her dress. She was escorted by her mother and oldest son Barry. All the ladies looked gorgeous in their gowns, but it was RJ who stole the show. He couldn't have been any cuter than he was on that day. Everything went as planned even though no one knew but a few of us that Brenda hired a security company to make sure that none of Robert's baby mamas came there with no drama. Well, everything went off without a hitch.

Everyone went to the country club for the cocktail hour and reception as the wedding party took pictures. It wasn't a long wait; and before everybody knew it, the bridal party was being introduced. Robert and Brenda walked in and had their first dance. I was so glad that they choose something that didn't have them grinding all over the place. The treat of the evening was when Robert danced with his mom Dell, and Brenda danced with RJ. I think everybody was tearing up. You could tell from Dell's expression that she was happy and proud to be dancing with her son. After the dance, he hugged and kissed her, and this caused her to start crying. She came over and hugged Momma and told her "thank you." Momma just smiled.

There was a photo booth, and everyone had fun taking pictures with the different props. The DJ they hired played something for everybody, and the dance floor stayed full.

Robert and Cindy left the reception after they toasted in the New Year as Mr. and Mrs. Robert Johnson. They left around 12:30 a.m., and the party started to thin out after that. I think that they had the place until 2:00 a.m., but Chris and I left right after Robert and Brenda. I was dog tired and wanted nothing but my bed. The next day, I slept until around ten which is very unusual for me. I'm usually up no later than seven, eight at the latest. Good thing we didn't have any children, or they would have starved. Sometimes I missed not having children, but it was a decision that both Chris and I agreed with. Chris was partner in a software company, and he was always traveling from one place to another. He said that he didn't want to be a part-time dad. He told me that now that I had retired, I could take some of these trips with him. Chris was a good man, one that I didn't take for granted. I was never lonely for children between Joyce's girls, Sam, and the students that I "adopted" at school. My life was complete.

By the time I had gotten up, Chris had made coffee and was already gone to play golf with the guys from work. I could tell that it was going to be one of those lazy days where I just lounge around and do nothing except relax and look at TV. Around midday, I showered, put on some clothes, and went back to the den. I knew that Chris would make a day of playing golf and would have dinner at the club with the guys.

Robert and Brenda went to Jamaica for their honeymoon. They spent a week there; and upon their return, they called me and thanked me for making their wedding a success. I told Robert that it was fun, but I had one request for him. "What is it, Cuz?" he asked.

"How about slow your roll and try your best to make this marriage work. Brenda really seems like a nice person."

"I know, and I promise you that I'm going to do my best."

Well, Cindy was back in her little world in Charlotte. I don't know what happened, but it seemed as if Cindy was getting her wish. Signs were beginning to surface, indicating that Paul had fallen off the wagon. Joyce said that she was seeing a lot of him in St. Paul lately, and the word on the street was that he had started using again. Damn! *This is all Cindy needs*, I thought to myself. If the rumors are true, she had Paul right back where she wanted him. Before long, Paul had lost his job, and they were moving back to St. Paul. Cindy was happy as a lark and felt that she was on top of the world.

Chapter 26

Cindy's Revenge

Cindy and I were talking again every day on the phone, but there was still something different about her. I just couldn't put my finger on it. Paul was trying to get a grip on reality before he was too far gone. I took it upon myself to invite Reverend Jamison and his wife down for dinner. I was hoping that he could reach him and help him get back on the right track. I told Reverend Jamison what was going on with Paul. I also invited Paul and Cindy, but I didn't tell them that Reverend and Mrs. Jamison would be there.

I knew that I was taking a risk by not telling Paul that Reverend Jamison would be here, but I was desperate. I couldn't stand the chance of losing Cindy again to the streets. When Cindy and Paul arrived, Reverend Jamison insisted on meeting them at the door. When he opened the door and Paul saw him, he just fell to his knees and started crying. He grabbed his leg and started begging Reverend Jamison to forgive him. "Get up, my son, and come in," he said. I could tell by Cindy's expression that she was none too pleased. Paul and Reverend Jamison were talking in Chris's office; and Cindy, Chris, Mrs. Jamison, and I were talking in the den.

Chris got a call from his partner, and Mrs. Jamison went to the restroom. That's when Cindy let me have it. "What the hell is wrong with you, Brett? You have lost your damn mind! What are you trying to do? I told you to stay out of my damn business!"

"I was beginning to worry about you," I defended.

"What do you mean worry about me? Did I ask for your fucking help? Answer me, bitch! Did I, in any way, ask for your fucking help, Brett?"

"No," I answered.

"You will regret this, bitch. Mark my word." She didn't get to say anymore because Mrs. Jamison was returning from the restroom. So we picked up our conversation from where we left off without missing a beat. It was hard to believe that this was the same Cindy that less than a minute ago was cussing me out.

Sue called us to dinner, and Chris went to get Reverend Jamison and Paul. As we were sitting down for dinner, Chris's partner, William, and his wife, Sheryl, stopped by on their way to dinner to bring some papers to Chris that he needed to read over and sign. We talked them into staying and joining us for dinner. The evening ended well. As everyone was saying their goodbyes and leaving, Paul hugged me and said, "Thank you. I needed this."

As Cindy left, she hugged me and whispered in my ear, "Remember what I said bitch!"

As Chris and I were settling in bed for the night, I gave him an account of the conversation between me and Cindy. I warned him to be careful because I don't know what she might try to do. Chris gave me the same warning.

Joyce and I had a nice long gossip fest the next morning. She couldn't believe what happened between me and Cindy. "Girl, you better be careful. You know that she's a crazy bitch." The next couple of weeks things were quiet on the home front. I didn't hear from or see Cindy; but I had my radar senses out because knowing Cindy, she was going to try and get me back.

Sure enough, she struck, and she struck hard. She went after Chris. I was glad that I warned him earlier to be careful. Well, she tried to set him up. She called him one day, saying that she needed him to help her with something at the house. He told her that he would come to St. Paul Saturday morning. When he got there, her girls were there, parading around half naked, some with just panties and no bras, others with short tops on and no panties. It just so happened that she wanted him to help her to assemble an entertainment center in her bedroom. "Come on now, Cindy girl, you are losing your touch." Most times, the men don't see it coming. Chris knew something was up when these girls started coming in and out the room, and they would happen to brush up against him or drop something that they had to pick up by him. Chris, not being as naive as she thought, played along with Cindy to see how far she was willing to go to get back at me. What Cindy didn't know was that Chris had called William on his way to Cindy's house and told him to meet him there. When William arrived, Cindy was furious! The two of them put the entertainment center together and left. When Chris told William what happened before he got there, they had a good laugh. Chris and William said, "That ain't no telling what Cindy and her friends would give you, probably something that you couldn't get rid of."

William followed Chris back to the house and came in and told me that I owed him big time for saving Chris from Cindy's trap. We had a good laugh about what happened and the look on Cindy's face when William showed up. That woman is a trip. When that attempt failed, Cindy didn't try anything else like that, and slowly she started testing the waters with me to see how I was going to react to her failed plot. I wasn't mad at Cindy because I know that she is a sick person and needs help, and this was a cry for help. She would call me like nothing happened, and we would talk like we always did. Then one day, out of the clear blue sky, she said, "Brett, I am sorry for what I tried to do to you and Chris. You know that I love you and Chris, and I would never do anything to hurt the two of you. I was just so upset with you, and I had to strike out at you. I know now that you care about me and was just looking out for my best interest."

"Girl, don't worry about it." Then I laughed and said, "Just don't do it again."

Laughing, she said, "Okay, bitch." *Cindy is back*, I thought.

Things just seemed to spiral from then. Chris was hurt in a freak accident at work. He almost died but with the grace of God, he pulled through. It was a long battle, but he made a full recovery. While he was recovering, I stepped in to help his partner, William, run the business. Luckily, it wasn't long before Chris was back to his old self again. Soon after returning to work, Chris and William decided to sell their business to a mega software company for 2.5 billion dollars in addition to keeping a 20% share of the company. Boy did we celebrate! Chris, William, his wife and I went on a month-long tour of Europe. It was fantastic! Chris even bought me my dream car, a fully loaded Bentley in my favorite color, blue.

Soon after that, Cindy started acting out again. By this time, she had gotten rid of Paul again and was taking her long trips without anyone knowing where she was. We knew that she would be back, so we would just sit by the phone and wait. She would call from time to time to let me know that she was all right. I would remind her to call Sam to let her know that she was all right. Sam would always call me to let me know that she had heard from her mother—good, at least she's thinking about Sam.

Chapter 27

Farewell

Then came that eerie call that morning. I'll never forget it as long as I live, just hearing the words "Cindy is dead," words that still haunt me to this day. Sam was too outdone. Her and her family came home and stayed with me. I hired a nanny to stay with the children so that she could handle the planning of the funeral and take care of business without having to worry about them being taken care of.

Nathan, Chris, and I helped her with the arrangements. Sam had the wake and visitation at her grandparents' house. The house was packed every day with people coming by to pay their respects. The night before the funeral, Sam wanted to spend the night at her grandparents' house. She asked if Chris and I would stay there with them. "Of course," I said. So I had dinner, brought in, and made arrangements with the restaurants to cater breakfast the next morning. The day of the funeral, the restaurant had a nice hot breakfast there bright and early. I knew that it was going to be a chore getting some food into them, but they needed to eat because it was going to be a long day. Joyce and the girls came over early to have breakfast and help in any way that they could. The day started off raining but turned into a beautiful day.

Before we knew it, the funeral director and the cars had arrived to take everyone to the church. Sam asked me, Chris, and Nathan to ride in the car with her, the children, and her husband. When we arrived at the church, I thought that I was going to be sick, but I got it together. I knew that I had to be strong for Sam's sake. As we walked in the church to take a final viewing of the body, there was a certain calmness about Cindy that I hadn't noticed before when I saw her body. She looked at peace with the world, and I knew that she was safe now because she was in a better place. I leaned in and told her that I loved her and that I was going to miss her, and I swear I heard her say, "Me too, bitch, me too."

Rest in peace, Cindy, rest in peace.

-The end-